If You Can't Get off the Horse You'd Better Learn to Ride

by Scott Weigle

Category: Self-Help

Market: Adult non-fiction

Publication Date: February 15, 2000

Specifications:

<u>Trim:</u> 5.5"x 8.5"	<u>Pages:</u> 224	<u>Price:</u> US $19.95
<u>Binding:</u> sewn 3-piece case		<u>Jacket:</u> full color
<u>ISBN:</u> 0-9670512-3-1		<u>LC:</u> 99-71756

Distributed by: Ingram, Baker and Taylor through ACCESS Publishers Network

Promotion: Web site, direct mail, e-mail, author tour

Contact:

Thomas-Kalland Publishers
Libby Barnes
PO Box 8376
Spokane, WA 99203-0376
Phone: (509)455-6867
Fax: (509)455-6858
E-mail: sabre5@earthlink.net

IF YOU CAN'T GET OFF THE HORSE YOU'D BETTER LEARN TO RIDE

If You Can't
Get off the Horse
You'd Better
Learn to Ride

Scott Weigle

THOMAS-KALLAND PUBLISHERS
Spokane

Cataloging-in-Publication Data

Weigle, Scott.
    If you can't get off the horse, you'd better learn to ride.
    p. cm.
    1. Conduct of life. 2. Success. I. Title.
BJ1581.2.W45   1999   158'.1 — dc20   99-71756
ISBN: 0-9670512-3-1

Printed and bound in the United States of America.

10 9 8 7 6 5 4 3 2 1

Look for this book at your favorite bookstore, or contact the
publisher directly to place an order. Letters to the author may
also be sent to this address.

Thomas-Kalland Publishers
PO Box 8376 / Spokane, WA 99203-0376
Toll Free: 800.788.5476 / Facsimile: 509.455.6858

To my wife, Betsy

You are the strength that binds me to the rest of the world,
and the love that sets me free.

ACKNOWLEDGMENTS

WRITING A BOOK is one thing you can accomplish all by yourself. In fact, having just finished one, I am able to confirm that the entire project can be completed without any human interaction at all . . . unless, of course, you plan to actually publish your work and have other people read it.

Once the decision has been made to share your thoughts with the world — which is really the point of writing in the first place — you have no choice but to involve others if you want to produce a worthwhile book. Many authors, myself included, are good at *writing*, but not so good at *reading*, especially if the words in front of them were produced by their own hand. Mistakes are missed time and again, and what seems crystal clear to the writer is sometimes, in reality, only a confusing muddle. It takes other people to point out the rough edges and encourage the author through the process of shaping and reshaping words until they communicate exactly the right thing. It's a long task, and I couldn't have done it alone. There are several people who helped me through it, and to them I owe a sincere debt of gratitude.

My parents provided three things that kept me going thoughout this long process: faith in my ability, belief in my dream and an example of what is possible once you decide to change your life. Their actions have truly been an inspiration, and their support and encouragement made all the difference. There were many people who expressed doubt about what I was trying to do—and the way I was going about it—but not them. For that I am grateful, but not surprised, since it was the same support they have given me throughout my life.

My editor, Chris Roerden, has provided invaluable assistance. Thankfully, she forgave all of my breaches of publishing etiquette and applied her extreme professionalism to every word of this text. Her pencil was quite sharp at times, but her words never were, and I emerged from the editing process a better writer than when I entered it.

Finally, and most importantly, I thank my wife, Betsy for her confidence in me and her countless hours of work on this book. Her patient guidance, clear insight and gentle but firm suggestions have had a significant impact on the development of these stories.

Thankfully, my wife saw in this book the same thing she saw in me when we first met: the promise hidden beneath the rough exterior. I have gained quite a bit of polish since we've been together, and she has continued to work her magic in all areas of my life, including my writing. Through her gentle efforts she brought out the best in this book, just as she has always brought out the best in me. For that, I am ever grateful.

CONTENTS

IF YOU CAN'T GET OFF THE HORSE YOU'D BETTER LEARN TO RIDE

UNEASY RIDER

DEEP IN THE HEART of every young boy lives the dream
of being a cowboy. It's a great dream, filled with adventure,
and I caught the excitement of it myself when I was about
ten years old. For a while, I wanted nothing more than to
spur a charging horse across an open prairie, feeling the
rush of the wind as I threw my lasso around the horns of a
runaway steer. I thought about my fantasy constantly, trying to figure out a way to make it come true.

The cowboy dream is a difficult one to turn into reality.
First, you've got to have a horse, and acquiring one can be a
big challenge to overcome. Next, you've got to know how to
ride, and that can be even harder. Although both sides of
my family had owned horses in the distant past, I didn't in-
herit a lot of natural riding skills; the family horses usually
pulled plows and wagons on my ancestors' farms, so they

didn't have to worry much about anyone jumping on their backs. My grandfather always said the Weigles were just not "horsey" people, and he was probably right.

Young boys, however, can be persistent dreamers. In spite of my family's history, my lack of a horse, and my not having the faintest idea of how to ride, I nevertheless wanted to be a cowboy. Although we'd never kept horses on the farm I grew up on, once I got the cowboy notion into my head I began to notice the creatures everywhere. We were surrounded by families with horses, and I saw no reason why the thunder of hooves shouldn't resound across our own land.

I approached Mom and Dad with my brother and sister. It was time to test the family bloodline, we told them; time to take a stab at being horsey. To our surprise, they agreed. Looking back, I now understand they had a plan all along. They recognized our desire to ride as a temporary childhood phase and knew it would pass more quickly if we got a taste of the real thing. Of course, seasoned parents that they were, they did not rush out and purchase a non-refundable horse. Instead, they borrowed one.

Suzy arrived early one spring.

I looked her over as she mowed down the grass in the small pen by the house. *Suzy,* I thought . . . *Suzy.* The name didn't fit the image of the charger I had been riding in my dreams. But she was white, or at least off-white, and therefore got the automatic distinction of being the mount of a "good guy." I decided I could live with that, in spite of her name. "I guess you'll do all right for this cowboy," I said, nodding at her.

Suzy raised her large head from the grass and looked me over, top to bottom: butch haircut, white T-shirt, faded jeans, hightop tennis shoes. *Doesn't look like a cowboy to me,* her large brown eyes said. *Kind of scrawny, in fact.* She snorted and tossed her mane. *This one shouldn't be too hard to get rid of!*

Suzy had been hanging around barnyards since before I was born, and she could smell an amateur rider a mile away. She knew every trick in the book and started intimidating me the first time I dragged the saddle over and heaved it onto her back. She expanded her belly dramatically and made painful-sounding whinnies as I tightened the cinch strap around her middle. Inexperienced in the ways of horses, I hesitated to make the large leather strap too snug for fear of hurting her. As soon as I stepped back to check my work, she snickered and let out her breath. The saddle suddenly looked a bit wobbly, but she flashed her large teeth at me. *Get on*, said the smile. *I'll be careful!*

I climbed into the saddle and looked around. The first thing I noticed was that a horse's back is a lot higher above the ground than I expected. Gingerly, I picked up the reins and tapped her flanks with my tennis shoes. She took one step. "Take it easy, girl!" I cautioned.

She stopped and looked back at me. *You've got to be kidding,* her eyes said. She did a snicker-snort thing and twitched her ears. *This kid's going to be easier to scare off than I thought!*

I nodded at her and she walked slowly around the barnyard, clip-clopping at a leisurely pace. "Relax!" Mom called out, watching from the end of the garden. "You look like you're not breathing." Breathing was one small detail I had been neglecting, and I let out a loud whoosh of air. Suzy startled, taking two quick steps. I panicked and dove forward, grabbing her neck in front of the saddle.

"Help!" I yelled, frantically looking around for Mom.

For some reason, Mom was wearing the same smile as Suzy, although she wasn't snorting. Not that I could hear, anyway. "Talk to her," she called out. "Let her know everything is all right."

"I'm okay, girl!" I said, thinking that was what Mom meant.

"Not you! Tell her *she's* okay! She doesn't care how you are."

Oh, I care, snorted Suzy, tossing her mane gleefully. *I care!*

I kept at it, walking Suzy slowly around the farm day after day. Gradually my confidence built and I began to feel I was the true master in this relationship. Suzy played along, even letting me tighten the saddle a notch or two without making that agonized expression she was so good at. After a couple days of walking, I had the courage to prod Suzy into a trot. She obliged, kicking up her hooves to make the ride as choppy as possible. It took me a while to learn the proper method of bouncing up and down in the same rhythm as the horse, but gradually the bruises on my bottom faded from purple to blue. *This horse stuff isn't so hard,* I thought as I put the saddle away one evening. I looked at the sunset and had a brief fantasy of riding off into it.

Once I had a few weeks of trotting under my belt, my confidence turned to pride. I could bounce in the saddle for an hour without showing a trace of fear. *Look at me,* I shouted in my mind, riding with one hand on my hip like they do in the movies. *I'm a cowboy!*

Look at him, said Suzy's eyes. *He's an idiot!*

I was ready for more speed. "Today's the day, Suzy-Q," I said cockily as I strapped on the saddle one afternoon. "I'm cinching this baby up tight because today we're really gonna ride!" I climbed aboard my trusty mount and urged her out of the barn and down the road to the pasture. She picked up the pace on her own, and I thought for a moment she must be excited about our adventure together. "Save your strength, girl. I'll let you go soon enough."

Suzy laid her ears back against her head. *You just make sure you're hanging on tight, little cowboy!*

4

Our small flock of sheep stopped grazing and looked up curiously as I opened the pasture gate. This was something new. They ambled over to the fence, out of the way, and settled down to chew their cud and watch the show. I aimed Suzy toward the far end of the pasture and coaxed her into a trot. *Once around should be sufficient for a warm-up*, I thought. I bounced by the sheep and they bleated at me. Even the spectators seemed to be catching the excitement.

On the home stretch back around to the gate I saw that my sister had appeared. *Maybe she's here to cheer me on*, I thought hopefully. Then I noticed Anne was accompanied by her friend, the neighbor girl from across the road. This girl was horsey in the truest sense of the word: she'd been born with a halter in her hand and she could tame a horse just by looking at it. I could have sworn she and Suzy exchanged winks as I rode by. *No problem. Cowboys don't worry about girls.*

"Here we go, baby!" I muttered through clenched teeth, being careful to keep my voice low so no one would think I was encouraging myself rather than the horse. I raised my tennis shoes and raked the dirty rubber soles across Suzy's flanks. Dust flew into the air as her hooves dug into the sandy soil, kicking up clumps of grass. I clutched the reins tightly in my sweaty palms as we moved into a fast trot. My jeans were sliding back and forth in the saddle and I tensed every muscle in my body to compensate. I took a deep breath and held it as I squeezed tighter with my knees and raked my shoes again.

Suzy tossed her mane twice and lowered her head. *You asked for it, cowboy. Your little rubber spurs are about to get you in trouble!*

Suzy kicked into full throttle and I hung on for dear life. We were going so fast I had to lean into the turn as we raced by the spectators on the next lap. Suzy seemed to be moving in all directions at once and the ride got bumpier. I imagined this roughness was sort of like the turbulence a jet encounters just before it breaks the sound barrier. I clutched even tighter, raked my tennis shoes one last time, and huddled low over the saddle horn as I'd seen jockeys do. My fate rested completely in the hands—or the hooves—of the runaway horse. Fence posts flashed by in a blur as I raced past the gate again, the wind trying to part my butch haircut. Feelings of exhilaration competed with the terror of falling under Suzy's hooves as my T-shirt flapped and my hightops curled around the stirrups. Suzy's body was a rippling machine of flexing muscle and thundering hooves. *Has anyone ever dared to push a horse this hard before?!* I wondered.

Gradually the fear of falling off subsided and the thrill of speed took over. I sat up a bit taller so I'd look good as I rode by my sister and I started to breathe again. I was on the verge of letting out a loud whoop for the benefit of the spectators when I sucked a bug into my throat. *Enough is enough,* I thought, choking and gasping. I had made my solo flight and proven my cowboy ability, at least to myself. Forgetting momentarily how to slow down my mount, I croaked "Stop . . . Halt . . . Whoa!" figuring one of them would work.

Suzy could have rightfully insisted on the standard signal of pulling back on the reins, yet she eased back into a trot, then slowed to a walk. The way she tossed her mane revealed her thoughts: *Mr. Hightops held on for only two laps! Maybe he should take up sheep riding!*

I composed myself as we proceeded back to the gate. Sitting up straight in the saddle, I stopped the horse by my sister and her friend. Suzy exchanged looks with the neighbor girl as if they had known each other for years. "Did you see that?!" I proudly exclaimed, trying to catch my breath. "I bet I was galloping faster than the pony express!"

The neighbor girl rolled her eyes at Suzy. "That wasn't a gallop," she stated matter-of-factly. "It was a canter."

"A 'canter?'" I wheezed. I'd never heard the term before.

"Yeah, a canter," she said. "A gallop is much faster."

"But," I protested, spitting out the last piece of bug, "I could barely stay on! That had to be a gallop."

"Well," she said, shrugging her shoulders, "you can call it a gallop if it makes you feel better. But it was canter. If you make room, I'll jump up there and show you a gallop."

Your move, cowboy! grinned Suzy, flaring her nostrils at me.

"Uh . . . I think I've scared the sheep enough for today," I stammered, having no intention of enduring any more laps around the pasture. "We'd better give them a break. Maybe later?"

Or never! snorted Suzy, prancing into a victory dance.

My horse ambitions had run their course. I probably rode Suzy once or twice more, but my heart wasn't in it. My brother and sister lost interest as well, just as my parents anticipated. Suzy soon went back to her permanent home, most likely refreshed from her brief holiday at the Weigle dude ranch.

For a long time after, I thought my horse-riding days were over. Somewhere along the way, however, about the time I turned thirty, I was struck with a sudden revelation. The scenery was starting to get blurry, the wind was picking up speed, and it dawned on me that I was back in the saddle again. This time the horse was my life, and Suzy had been tame by comparison.

Although I hadn't realized it, I had actually been riding for a long time. A pace that started out at an easy walk in my youth had gradually picked up speed as I left my small town for college. Marriage and military service followed, and I was too busy trying to figure out the rhythm of the bumps to notice I was definitely trotting. Several years and one child later, I found myself in the civilian world again, dealing with a new career, a new home, and everything else that comes with starting over. That's about the time I realized my life had turned into a ride on a runaway horse, and that I had become an unsteady cowboy at a canter once again. The canter felt as rough as the last time I had experienced it, and I was no longer alone—this time I had to keep a whole family balanced on a loose saddle.

It didn't stop there. I was no longer in the familiar surroundings of our pasture; instead, I found myself competing with other riders in the frantic race of modern life, sucking in bugs and trying to take hold of the reins as the pace continued to pick up. My second child was the final spur, and finally I understood how a full gallop really felt. Simply hanging on became my primary concern. I began asking myself questions: *What am I doing? Where am I heading?* And the big one: *If my life is a horse, how do I make it go where I want it to go?*

I began looking back at my experiences and discovered the stories from my past had already taught me everything I needed to know. I simply had to learn how to apply my knowledge in order to slow down and gain control over my direction in life. The self-styled riding lessons I had begun as a young boy picked up once again with a renewed sense of purpose. This time I couldn't stop the horse and take a break. This time I couldn't get off.

This time I had no choice—I had to learn to ride.

THE NATURAL ORDER OF THINGS

"IS THAT YOUR CAT?"

The loud voice caught my wife by surprise as she paused on the front porch, hand in the mailbox. She turned and saw a young man across the street, holding a notepad and pointing earnestly at the front sidewalk. The object of his attention was lying calmly on the warm concrete, licking his paws and ignoring the rest of the world.

The words sounded like an accusation as he repeated them: "Is that your cat?!"

Betsy knew the answer, yet she hadn't been expecting the question. She managed a soft "um," but wasn't sure where to go from there.

The man started across the street, jogging to beat a passing car. As he hopped onto the curb in front of our house, he repeated his question again. "Ma'am! Is that your cat?"

Startled out of his daydream, our cat leapt to his feet and raced to the porch, uncharacteristically rubbing his sleek, black coat against the protection of my wife's legs.

"Who are you?" Betsy finally managed as the insistent young man stepped up to the porch. Our cat was pushing against the partly open front door, trying to force his way inside.

"Animal control, ma'am," he stated, sounding official in spite of his lack of a uniform. He opened his notepad. "I'm here to verify your cat license."

Cat license? Suddenly she understood. Probably on the basis of an expensive study, our city council had concluded that a large cat population was enjoying the benefits of city services without paying for them. Naturally, such a large source of potential revenue could not go untapped, and the council had recently decreed that all cats be licensed at the rate of seven dollars per year. The decision was widely regarded in the community as an attempt to control the uncontrollable. The city would have had better luck trying to regulate squirrels — like cats, squirrels don't come when you call them, but at least they'll look.

Normally we weren't lawbreakers, yet we had not rushed out to purchase the required cat license. Apparently the city had anticipated the low compliance rate and had deputized animal control officers to round up the renegade felines and touch their recalcitrant owners with the long arm of the law. One such bounty hunter now stood smiling greedily over the fee our cat would generate for being caught red-handed, or pawed, as the case may be.

He repeated his question a final time: "Is that your cat?"

You mean this one that's trying to force its way into my house? thought my wife. Our cat usually acted aloof, but true to his unpredictable nature, he was at that moment the very picture of an affectionate and loving pet. He purred loudly and continued to push against the front door.

"Well, he's not acting like my cat," Betsy finally managed to say. "Does that count?"

As she wrote out the check for the license and fine, she asked herself the same thing: *Is that my cat?* The question was definitely a good one, and based on our relationship with the feline in question, it could not be easily answered.

Willy had joined our family as our first child. Shortly after marriage, my wife and I had packed up our worldly possessions and driven across the country to my first Army assignment. I was there for several months of Infantry training, a career field requiring extended periods of time collecting ticks in the pine forests of Fort Benning, Georgia. Separated from our families by a dozen or more states, we had only each other for company, and it was difficult for Betsy when I left for weeks in the field. The time had come for a pet.

The thought occurs to me that I was being replaced by a cat. In any event, as with so many decisions in the lives of young couples, we proceeded without giving real thought to the possible consequences of our actions. This is the same approach that got us into trouble a few years later with children.

We visited a pet store at the mall to research the availability of cats. Inside a large wire cage a dozen or so kittens frolicked playfully, rolling together over their food dishes and batting at each other. No two were alike, and a cat could be found to match any decor. We spent the next week talking over our options and agreed to look for a white cat, maybe with brown or gray spots across the back. Ready for the commitment, we headed back to the mall.

We could see from the doorway the cage was empty. Disappointed, we asked the clerk if he had any kittens left. He pointed to the cage and told us to look closely. Inside, down in the corner behind a rubber toy, crouched a tiny kitten, his fuzzy black coat nearly lost in the shadows. Black hadn't been one of our choices.

"Are there any others?" we asked hopefully.

The only other available kitten was in a separate cage along the wall, isolated, apparently, because of his wild behavior. A gray tabby, several weeks old, he was climbing the sides of the cage and chewing on the wire. He seemed too aggressive for our tastes, so we turned once again to look at the black puff of fur. He wasn't jumping around like the tabby; in fact, he wasn't moving at all.

My wife held him up for closer inspection. He fit in the palm of her hand and weighed only a few ounces. Turning him around a few times, she noticed he had a flea sticking off his chin. He wasn't what we had in mind, and Betsy was about to put him back and suggest we return the next weekend when the pitiful little animal turned his face to stare directly into her eyes. Opening his tiny mouth, he issued a barely audible noise. A week of careful cat planning and analysis went out the window with one tiny "mew." Willy came home with us that day.

Willy's unique personality didn't take long to surface. He refused to eat anything for three days, and appeared to be on a hunger strike. We tried several varieties of cat food to tempt him, without success. On the fourth day, Betsy sat down to eat a bowl of instant mashed potatoes and immediately had a cat in her lap. He ate half the bowl, and mashed potatoes forever remained one of his favorite foods.

At first we congratulated ourselves on choosing the cat with the calm demeanor. Within a few weeks, however, we discovered a kitten's calmness is a function of its small size, and as the size increases, so does the energy. Soon Willy could jump three feet straight up and wad a large throw rug into a ball in less than a minute. The cat who was supposed to be Betsy's constant companion quickly became her constant aggravation.

Knowing we would be moving a lot in the Army, our original intention had been to train Willy to be strictly an indoor cat. From the beginning, Willy had other ideas. Within a few weeks, he discovered windows and understood he was missing out on a lot of the world. The second time he climbed to the top of the screen door, my wife had all she could take. In exasperation, she opened the door and he shot across the yard like a black comet, disappearing into the woods behind our house.

"I have given the cat his freedom," Betsy called me at work to report. "And I don't care if he ever comes back."

Four hours later I found myself searching the woods with a flashlight, a tearful wife walking close behind, chastising herself for turning her baby loose into the cruel world. There was no sign of Willy. I assured her the cat would be fine.

My convictions faded the next day when he didn't return, and that night we drove the highway behind our house, looking for scraps of fur at the side of the road. Now I felt miserable, too.

The following day we gave up, feeling we had betrayed the first life to count on us in the world. Betsy opened the door to call his name one last time and there he sat on the patio. He stretched and strolled inside, apparently having decided he'd had enough fun with us.

"He's home!" she announced happily to me on the phone. The prodigal cat had returned and we showered him with affection.

Round one to Willy. He became an indoor-outdoor cat and proved himself capable of handling any of the ten apartments and houses we eventually lived in. He seemed to have an instinct for finding his way home no matter what the circumstances, a skill probably based on the location of his food dish.

Transporting Willy from one house to another was never simple. When I transferred from Georgia to Kansas, the trip took two-days on the freeway, so Willy got his own area in the back seat: a cozy arrangement of food, water, and litter box. Everything started off fine, and on the open road he was a model traveler, snoozing for hours in the back window among the house plants.

Somewhere in Tennessee, we found ourselves driving through the first big city. We pulled out the map to locate our position in the maze of freeways, and Willy decided to participate in the navigation process. As we wove in and out of traffic, he alternated between standing on the driver's lap with paws on the wheel, and sprawling in the middle of the map. After a close call with a large truck, we forced him off the seat and he found a spot he liked under the brake pedal. We ejected him from that position as we hit the twisting maze of interchanges in the city center, and he sulked in the back seat. The last laugh belonged to him, however. Upset over our lack of appreciation, he proceeded to put the litter box to its intended use. Frantically we rolled down our windows, only to lose our map in the rush of wind. This pattern repeated itself as we drove through each city on the trip, and on each trip thereafter, until we got smart enough to purchase a cat carrier.

Every one of our houses has a Willy story, most of them revolving around his taste for freedom. After losing the fight to make him an indoor cat, we figured he'd be happy as long as he could go outside. In reality, he was happy only if he could go outside whenever the mood struck him. He insisted on having the same rights Betsy and I had as family members, and it became common practice for us to open and close the door for the cat three dozen times a day.

At one house I had the brilliant idea of installing a cat door. This led to our first notice that Willy, now an adolescent, was hanging out with a bad crowd. Worse still, we discovered he liked to invite them over to visit. I learned this late one night when I felt paws on my stomach and awoke to find myself staring into the fluorescent yellow eyes of a large cat.

"Willy?" I said hopefully.

The cat immediately extended four sets of claws and leaped to the floor. In the dim light from the window, I could identify the intruder as the neighbor's huge, mutant gray cat. This animal was such a rough character he scared me in broad daylight. Each morning I watched him as he sat outside our dining room window, grooming himself by running his claws through his hair backward and licking the scars on his chest. And now he was loose in my house, at night. I wasn't thrilled.

The gray cat ran downstairs and I cautiously tip-toed after him, forgetting to put on my glasses in the confusion. Every shadow looked cat-shaped. "Here kitty, kitty." Not a sound. Flicking on the light, I saw him sharpening his teeth on the edge of the refrigerator. I eased open the front door, stood back, and said, "Shoo!"

The gray cat leered at me and flashed what appeared to be a tattoo on one of his biceps. He casually walked over to Willy's dish and swallowed the food in one gulp, then sauntered out the door without any sign of fear. Pausing on the step, he raised his paw and snapped his claws. Willy raced out the door between my legs, joining his unsavory friend on another late-night adventure.

The cat door came out that night.

Our family photo album steadily filled with pictures of Willy. His all-black coloring didn't lend itself to photographs, and he usually formed a black blob with yellow eyes in every picture, no matter what the background. That didn't stop us; as with children and a camera, we wanted to catch him in the act of doing everything. He wasn't difficult to pose, and most of the pictures had a common theme: Willy asleep on the fence; Willy asleep in the sewing box; Willy asleep on the back of the couch. Like most cats, he elevated napping to an art form.

Yet things happen when you're married, and Willy was entering young adulthood when he found his napping schedule interrupted by the birth of our first child. Suddenly there was competition for everything; sunny spots and solitude were hard to claim, and attention came at a premium. Willy took the development in stride, acting as if he thought our fascination with this new pet in diapers would gradually fade.

Within a few years, the second child came along and Willy could tell he would be sharing his space with the intruders permanently. He perfected his long-term strategy of acting disinterested and aloof on the subject of children. He also displayed a sense of humor; he began to nap in the middle of rooms or in doorways, spots that forced us to step over him so we would be constantly reminded our daily average of sleep had dropped to one-tenth of what he experienced. I once counted up his waking hours and calculated his actual day was two-thirds shorter than ours. His unspoken motto seemed to be: "If the situation gets bad enough, go to sleep. It will probably be over when you wake up."

Although Willy preferred to ignore the small humans, he couldn't avoid involvement; in due time, he became one of three-year-old Robby's obsessions. More precisely, the obsession was to "give kitty a bath." Kitty didn't like baths—he rarely even gave himself a lick—yet nothing stopped Robby from trying to accomplish his mission. For several months it became a common sight to see him staggering through the house carrying the cat, headed for the only bathtub he could reach: the toilet.

We were usually successful in stopping the fun before things got out of hand, and Willy was never in serious danger of getting his feet wet. Have you ever tried to force a cat, claws and all, into a toilet? Take it from my son: it's hard work, and a person would have to be much older and stronger than a three-year-old to have even a slight chance of success. Still, Willy could do without the game, and he seemed relieved when Robby moved on to other fascinations.

Shortly after the kids entered the scene, pictures of Willy began to grow scarce in the photo album. He was still visible, but generally in the background, sitting behind laughing birthday party guests or trying to avoid a squirt gun fight. On the surface, it appeared Willy was being pushed from the scene.

However, perseverance wins most wars, if not individual battles, and Willy had patience in abundance. He knew he would eventually achieve what he wanted by waiting, an activity made easier by spending most of his day asleep. His time would come again, one way or another. Besides, the important things in life were being taken care of: fresh catnip in the garden, people to let him in and out, and his own bowl of mashed potatoes at Thanksgiving and Christmas. *It's not undivided attention,* he probably reasoned, *but the perks are still pretty decent.*

Then came the dog. To make matters worse, the dog spent much of her time in the house. She appeared to be the biggest challenge yet to Willy's position in the household; not only did she take up valuable napping space on the floor, she begged constantly for attention. Willy definitely drew the line at begging, yet in a family with two children and a dog, begging is often a prerequisite for getting any attention at all.

Our world had changed a lot since we had first set out on our own, and Willy's little part of that world had changed as well. Our lives had gotten much more complex—maybe too complex for even a cat to control.

Or so I thought.

One summer night the real pecking order became clear as I experienced a familiar ritual: dessert. I was popping corn, and a small flurry of activity surrounded me at the stove. Both kids hopped up and down excitedly to the pinging of exploding kernels hitting the lid of the pot, and the dog balanced on her haunches, begging for a taste. Quietly, calmly, Willy sat curled out of harm's way in the dining room, occasionally peering through one half-open eye at the show in the kitchen. The spectacle had undoubtedly been repeated countless times since cats first domesticated man.

Imagine a similar scene from the distant past: early man hunches over a cooking fire at the mouth of a cave, hanging strips of meat on sticks. Children, their faces smudged from a day of playing in the dirt, hop up and down to the sound of sizzling fat dripping onto the coals, and a dog begs intently for a scrap of anything. Quietly and calmly, a primeval cat sits curled out of harm's way in the shadows of the cave; begging for scraps does not cross its mind. It knows the real benefits of keeping humans around are a result of patience, and eventually it will get the attention it deserves. Meanwhile, a nap is in order.

Sure enough, as the sun drops behind the mountains, the dog is exiled to the cold rocks outside the cave to gnaw on a bone and the kids are tucked under a woolly mammoth hide with stern orders to stay put. The cat opens its eyes, stretches, rises and stares intently at the human. On cue, perhaps without knowing what compels him to do so, the caveman tosses over a piece of meat. Secure in the warmth of the cave, the cat feasts in solitude, untroubled by hopping kids and drooling dogs. No bedtime for this early feline, just the run of the cave until sunrise.

Dog on the back porch, kids upstairs in bed, I thought about this scenario as I placed a handful of liver-flavored treats in front of Willy. Who was kidding whom? Willy's position of control had never been threatened. It's results that count, and nothing had changed since the cat first came home with us; he was still living his own life, doing whatever he wanted, and eating special treats hand-delivered by humans.

No, Willy never lost his place; it simply took time for the rest of the family to find theirs. As the kids grew out of infancy, Willy and I grew further into adulthood. Slowly, a pattern emerged usually found between old friends. Seeking an hour or two of quiet in a house with children, I became an early riser, and each morning Willy awaited me. First came treats. Then, as I sat writing, his purring kept me company. Our hours alone before the sunrise became our time together, and no one—not the kids, not the dog—disturbed us. I slowly realized the kids and the dog had to be taken care of, but the cat could handle himself. I grew to enjoy our mornings together, Willy and me.

Betsy reported a similar development in her own relationship with the cat. Willy, whom we had originally brought home to keep her company, was still with her in quiet moments.

"Is that your cat?" the impatient young man had asked.

After due consideration, the answer would have to be, "Not exactly. He lives here, but he is definitely not *ours*." That's an important distinction, especially when a cat is involved. He'd had us under his spell from the moment we first set eyes on him; it simply took us a while to figure out that Willy had always called the shots. Seven dollars for a cat license? Our city council had things backward: with a bit more thought on the issue, they would have realized it was more appropriate to charge cats for human licenses.

Not that a cat would ever pay for the privilege of keeping humans around. It was just the natural order of things.

❖　　　❖　　　❖

RIDING LESSON:

Very few days cannot be improved by a nap.

FIRE IN THE CABIN

THE DAY HADN'T STARTED out cold. In fact, it had been warm enough for an overnight hike. That's how weather goes in the mountains, though—all too often the beautiful face of a new morning turns ugly by noon, especially when fall is starting to act more like winter and you are rushing to complete the last hike of the year. I had seen the situation more than once in my short career as a Boy Scout, and the consequences of such a sudden drop in the temperature were never good.

"Load 'em up boys." Mr. Weldon hoisted his backpack onto his knee, then rotated his arms through the straps. "The rest stop is over. We've got to make it to camp before the wind gets much colder."

Mr. Weldon was no stranger to the forces of change. As Scoutmaster of Troop 141, he supervised a bunch of adolescent boys who were prone to unpredictable behavior. In my mind, he set the perfect example of strong leadership, and I thought he could handle anything. Yet the challenges of this hike had just begun, and Mr. Weldon's abundant patience was to be tested severely before the next sunrise.

One of the other adults led the line of boys up the winding trail while Mr. Weldon brought up the rear to keep an eye on stragglers. Our destination was an old, abandoned mining camp called Boulder City, nestled high in the mountains of central Idaho. I zipped my coat to my chin to ward off the relentless wind and tightened the straps on my backpack. *It's getting colder by the minute,* I thought.

As if to confirm my thoughts, a voice sounded behind me. "Man, I'm freezing." The words came from one of the newest scouts in our troop, an intense sixth-grader by the name of Renny Woodman. "I'm starting to feel like a popsicle." When I didn't respond he smacked my backpack. "How about you, Wiggle?"

I sighed. I felt too cold to be concerned with anyone else, yet I knew Renny wouldn't allow himself to be ignored. "Yeah, me too," I replied.

This was only Renny's second hike with our troop, but he had already made his mark. In fact, he had been given a nickname to match his personality. On his first hike, one boy had noticed Renny Woodman possessed a rather long and pointy nose, and that he continually poked it into everyone's business. One of the older scouts picked up on the comment and joked that we should call him Renny Woodpecker. The moniker may have been intended to be cruel, yet Renny loved it, and repeated the name over and over. Soon, he began mimicking woodpecker movements with his head and cracking bird jokes to anyone who would listen. By the time we packed up to return home from his first outing, the nickname had evolved, through constant repetition, into a shortened form that fit him perfectly. Renny himself had made the announcement to the entire troop as we prepared to leave. From that point forward, he stated, he would answer only to "Renpecker." Mr. Weldon hadn't been thrilled, but the scouts loved the name, so it stuck.

I turned and glanced at him as we rounded a corner on our steady traverse up the mountain. "You better put a hat on, Renpecker," I warned him. "Your ears are turning red."

"Yeah, I know." He cupped his hands over them. "Didn't bring a hat, though." He looked troubled for a moment, then brightened. "I know! I'll tie a sock around them." He stopped in the middle of the trail and turned around. "Dig a pair out of my pack for me, okay?"

I shook my head as I helped him. Planning ahead wasn't Renpecker's strong suit, a failing that had gotten him into more than one difficult situation.

"Woodman!" the Scoutmaster yelled from the end of the line. "What are you doing up there? Get moving!"

"Whoops," said Renpecker as he staggered up the trail, trying to walk and tie a green sock around his head at the same time. "The Weld-man is getting cranky."

A tired bunch of boys and men stumbled into camp hours later. The wind had turned colder as the trail grew steeper near the top, and the effects of the rapidly falling temperature were evident in our shuffling steps. The last rays of the setting sun cast dark shadows among the ramshackle cabins and abandoned machinery of the old mining camp. There would be a lot of exploring to do tomorrow. For now, however, we simply craved sleep.

We dumped our gear in a pile and collapsed. We were too tired to eat, so Mr. Weldon set up a backpacking stove and began boiling water for hot chocolate. As we sat warming ourselves with cups of instant cocoa, I noticed that even Renpecker seemed fatigued.

That's unusual, I remember thinking to myself, *but it probably won't last long.* I was right.

The cocoa tasted good, and we sat quietly, gulping down cup after cup. We emptied the pot and put another one on, and then a third. A half hour passed before Mr. Weldon extinguished the stove and sat back. "Listen up, boys. You're going to bed down tonight in this old cabin behind me." He jerked his thumb at the large structure he was leaning against. It was missing its doors and windows, and there were several good-sized holes in the roof. "The floorboards are rotted out, so you'll be able to roll your sleeping bags out between the floor beams. That should keep you out of the worst of the wind."

He paused and looked at each of us in turn to emphasize his next words. "And tonight, I want you to go straight to bed." His gaze came to rest on Renpecker. "And that means two things: none of your usual messing around, and no campfires."

"What?!" Renpecker's shriek could be heard clearly over the howling wind. His fatigue had vanished. "If we don't have a fire we'll die!"

Mr. Weldon had expected resistance from his most challenging subject. In a weary yet firm voice he repeated, "Absolutely no fires tonight, Woodman. It's too late and everybody needs their rest. Go to bed."

Renpecker was aghast. "But ... but ... we'll freeze to death!"

He definitely has a point there, I thought, shivering as I clutched a stainless steel cup in my cold fingers. *A fire would be kind of nice.*

With the many unique aspects to Renpecker's personality, it would be hard to choose a single defining characteristic. Yet if pressed to select only one thing setting the active young boy apart, you would have to say this: Renpecker had a thing for fires. For him, it was more than simple attraction—the feeling was strong enough to be called love.

To be fair, Renpecker was not alone in his fascination. All scouts, to one degree or another, love to build fires. The reasons for this can be understood only if one remembers scouts share the common trait of being boys, and young boys are fascinated by flame. Since scouts in the wild have the unspoken permission to build fires and throw nearly anything combustible upon them, they are extremely reluctant to give up any opportunity to act on this fascination.

As I watch my own boys today, sneaking green leaves into the barbecue to watch the smoke curl up through the burger patties, I sometimes think I'm seeing a prehistoric instinct at work. Fire was the most significant tool savage man possessed, and as he learned to control its properties it became the very symbol of his mastery over the environment. Since boys have a touch of the savage in their basic nature, perhaps they can't help themselves—they simply love to mess with fires.

Renpecker had turned "messing with fires" into an art form. There wasn't a plant in the forest, dead or alive, he hadn't torched at least once. He had been looking forward to a campfire so much he had been collecting sticks to burn as he made his way up the mountain. But the Scoutmaster wasn't in the mood to argue, and his position was final.

We poured one last round of cocoa, and by the time it disappeared we couldn't hold another drop. We stacked our backpacks outside the cabin, tied a tarp over them, rolled out our sleeping bags between the floor beams, and crawled in. We dozed off, listening to the howl of the wind whistling through the missing windows of the cabin.

An hour later I awoke from an uneasy sleep to a loud ripping noise. "What was that?" said a voice near me in the darkness. Several of us sat up, and saw pieces of fabric flapping outside the window. The wind had picked up enough speed to rip in half the tarp that was covering our backpacks.

"Does anyone smell smoke?"

I turned to look toward one of the doors, and the source of the smell became immediately obvious. Orange flames danced in the shadows, illuminating a green sock flapping from a nail in the cabin wall. *Renpecker disobeyed orders!* I thought in shock. *He started a fire!*

Yet that wasn't the worst. Apparently he had been having trouble getting the fire lit in the roaring wind, so he had built it in the only calm spot he could find — under the door frame. Now the flames were crawling up the sides of the door, and Renpecker, his short attention span as exhausted as his skinny body, was nowhere to be found. Unfortunately, as excited as he was about starting fires, he lacked a corresponding desire to put them out. He had finally been overcome by sleep and crawled off into the deep shadows of the large cabin.

"Renpecker!" I called out in alarm. "Renpecker!"

The rest of the boys in the troop were awake, and they joined in. *"Renpecker!"* No answer, and nothing stirred in the shadows.

"RENPECKER!"

It was no use; after the exhausting hike and his nocturnal fire-building, his collapse had been total. He simply refused to wake up.

We all agreed the fire was neither our fault nor our responsibility, and absolutely no good reason existed for us to crawl out of our sleeping bags to handle it. Our position was logical, except for one indisputable fact: the fire was burning down the same cabin we were sleeping in.

Our lack of action was not unusual; the first thing most people do when faced with serious change, unfortunately, is ignore it in the hope it will go away. This is simply human nature, yet ignoring change doesn't work for long. The next step is to do as little as possible and pray the situation works itself out. Sometimes luck prevails and the problem ends there. If it doesn't, if the change is too big to go away on its own, there's only one thing left to do. As I was to learn on that cold, dark night many years ago, the only way to handle serious change is to face it head-on and take decisive action.

As the fire began to lick at the wall above the door, our anger at Renpecker slowly gave way to a dawning realization: the situation may be unfair, but if we didn't want to become Boy Scout toast we would have to save our own skins. Our first response—yelling at Renpecker—hadn't worked. What next? A careful observer would have immediately recognized the need for water in such a situation; a few bucketfuls would have made short work of the flames. Yet if that same observer had been at the scene with us, poking his head into the howling wind, he would have immediately spotted the flaw in his reasoning: the night was freezing cold. The wind chill, we agreed by consensus after sticking our fingers into the air, had dropped to dozens of degrees below zero.

We briefly considered a bucket brigade, but we also considered that the nearest water was over five hundred feet away in the creek and covered with ice. Normally, that wouldn't have posed too much of a problem, but we had all made a fateful decision before turning in. As we were unrolling our sleeping bags, a young scout had raised the question of how best to stay warm. Thus began an age-old debate, carried out by campers for generations: how much clothing should one wear to bed?

There was always a group of scouts that swore by sleeping in everything, including boots. They were usually accused of simply being lazy, and the description probably fit. The moderates always insisted a particular outfit of underwear, shirts, and socks would provide the best results, and the precise combination had to be determined by the prevailing weather conditions at sunset. That night, however, we had fallen under the influence of a radical group advocating the position of camping purists. Our powers of reasoning must have been numbed by cold and fatigue, because we had all succumbed to the myth that you sleep warmer if you sleep naked.

Hence, in the middle of that cold night, the creek wasn't seriously considered. Yet we knew we had to do something. What would a reasonable person do, given the constraints we were working under? We lay there for a while, pondering and watching the flames crawl up the wall, until someone spoke up. "Man, how long has it been since we drank all that hot chocolate?"

The question started a chain of reasoning bound to lead to trouble among a group of boys. Gradually, we realized an hour had passed since each of us, individually, had drunk close to a quart of the beverage. Maybe, we reasoned, we did have a source of liquid a lot closer than the creek. I'm not sure who first voiced the option out loud, but soon everyone agreed: if we had to get up anyway, we could in effect kill two birds with one stone.

To our credit, we did hold a short debate on how we could best justify our actions. We were stumped for a few minutes, until someone remembered the Boy Scout motto, which seemed to fit the situation perfectly: Be prepared!

I cannot comment further on our courageous attempt to extinguish the fire except to say two things: the wind was very cold, and our plan didn't work. We had expended the minimal effort possible in the hope the situation would work itself out, thereby employing the classic second step used by so many people after simply ignoring the situation doesn't work. At best, our plan amounted to a half-hearted way to deal with a serious problem. As the last scout crawled back into his sleeping bag, the flames made a sudden leap to the rafters and began to advance over our heads.

As things stood, we were only minutes from becoming fuel for a rapidly expanding inferno. If we delayed much longer, our nylon sleeping bags would begin to melt, transforming us into giant, multi-colored, toasted marshmallows. Having tried everything we could think of without success, we were left with the need for drastic measures: in spite of potential repercussions, we decided the Scoutmaster had to be told.

We were hesitant to expose our bare essentials to the wind chill factor again, so getting out of bed wasn't considered. Instead, we screamed as loudly as we could from our prone positions, "Fire in the cabin!" No response. Again: "Fire in the cabin!" Nothing could be heard except the howling of the wind and the crackling of the flames. After a pause, someone suggested our calls for help might work better if we sat up above the floor beams and faced toward the leaders' cabin. This seemed reasonable, and didn't require too much extra effort or exposure to the cold. As a group, we waited for the wind to shift to the right direction, then yelled as loudly as we could: "Mister Weldon! Help! Mister Weldon! There's a fire in the cabin! FIRE IN THE CABIN!"

His door slammed open, and moments later he arrived. He had gotten dressed so quickly his boots were unlaced and his pants were on backwards. He paused at the door opposite the source of the fire and sized up the scene. In his tenure as Scoutmaster, Mr. Weldon had seen the entire range of activities kids were capable of, from slightly foolish to downright stupid. This topped them all. Looking up, he saw a fire burning the length of the cabin and spreading rapidly from rafter to rafter. Looking down, he saw several rows of silent scouts, tucked into their sleeping bags and smiling at him innocently as they tried to ignore the hot cinders and ashes falling around them.

With the flames reflecting from his wide-open eyes and his voice rising above the howling wind, he screamed out, "What are you idiots doing?!"

Mr. Weldon didn't wait for an answer, which was fine since we didn't have one. Instead, he sprang into action. Acting swiftly, he grabbed the first sleeping bag he came to and dumped out the occupant. He shoved a pot from a cook kit at the shocked and shivering scout and yelled, "To the creek, you nitwit! Run!"

The rest of us suddenly realized we were caught between a raging fire and a crazed Scoutmaster, an extremely dangerous position to be in. We quickly decided we would be much safer outside the cabin, in spite of the cold. We leaped up, grabbed our own cook kits, and dashed off toward the creek, with Mr. Weldon in hot pursuit. He chased us to the creek and back several times as we raced through the freezing darkness, carrying small pots of water mixed with chunks of ice. Even Renpecker couldn't sleep through such a commotion, and he joined in the fun about half-way through. Although we were cursing his name at every step, he became so caught up in the excitement he never realized he was the cause of the problem.

Within minutes the fire had been reduced to ashes. We stood in the old cabin, gasping, wheezing, shivering, and knowing we had learned an unforgettable lesson on dealing with change. If ignoring the situation doesn't work, if doing as little as possible doesn't work, you have no choice but to go to the final step: facing the circumstances head-on and taking decisive action.

Personally, I learned one other lesson that night, something I could put to use on future camping trips. I learned that when you bed down under the stars with a group of boys, there's no telling what's going to happen during the night. And when the temperature falls below freezing, it is much, much, *much* better to *not* be sleeping naked.

❖   ❖   ❖

Riding Lesson:

Many people deal with change like an ostrich—
they put their heads in the sand and hope life doesn't kick
the part left sticking out.

THE ROSE

"HI, GRAMPA."

"Well, hello, Scott." My grandfather straightened up from the rose bush he was working on. "I thought you were playing down in the basement."

My face crinkled into a squint in the hot glare of the August sun. "I was, but I wanted to see what you were doing."

He nodded and held up a pair of nippers. "I'm trimming up my roses. Would you like to help?"

"Sure," I said eagerly. "What can I do?"

"You bring along that fertilizer." He pointed toward a metal can. "After I'm done trimming, you can sprinkle a little around each plant." I picked up the can and watched him closely, waiting for his nod before shaking out some fertilizer on the first rose.

His name was William Weigle, but everyone called him Bill. My father's father, he was a tall man — at least to my six-year-old eyes — and he always dressed the same: dark trousers sharply creased down the front, and neatly pressed plaid shirts. Today he had on short sleeves, but when winter came he would wear long-sleeved wool. Grampa always wore a hat, too: a fedora made of felt with a silk band during the cold months, and one made of straw when the weather turned hot. He smiled a lot, his kind eyes crinkling behind black-rimmed glasses. From a young age I had often been told I looked a lot like both my father and my grandfather, and that always made me feel proud.

Although I often visited Grandma and Grampa's house with my brother and sister, on this day I had come alone, dropped off by my mother to spend a long summer afternoon. For lunch Grandma had made egg salad sandwiches and vegetable soup. After eating, I had gone down to the basement to play with the old Lincoln Logs that used to belong to my father when he was a boy. I loved to build miniature cities on the concrete floor and drive Dad's old tin cars through them. I had gotten lonely after a while, though, and had gone in search of Grampa, knowing I would find him in his rose garden.

Grampa's hands moved with a skill that came from decades of experience. We made our way up and down the rows of bushes, working mostly in silence among the sweet perfume of many dozen blooms. Grampa expertly trimmed back a few stems on each rose, then held the thorny canes out of the way while I shook out a few grains of fertilizer. After about a half hour we reached the last plant.

"Looks like we're done, Scott," he said with an approving nod. "Thanks for your help."

I put the lid back on the can. "Sure."

He slipped his nippers into his pocket. "All this hard work makes a man thirsty. Let's go ask your Grandma for a glass of ginger ale." We walked together across the patio toward the house, and as he opened the screen door he put his hand on my shoulder. "You did a good job, Scott. I can tell that you're going to be a fine gardener some day."

I smiled up at him. "Thanks, Grampa."

My grandparents had been living in their house for almost thirty years by the time of my first childhood visits. To me, their home always seemed calm, orderly, and peaceful, a place where everything—inside and out—was perfectly arranged. The place didn't change much as I grew up, which was fine by me because I liked it the way it was.

They lived in a one-story house painted white with dark gray shutters. Shaded by towering maple trees, it was enclosed by perfectly trimmed green hedges and surrounded with beds of bright flowers. Their back patio looked out over a lawn kept manicured by careful mowing and edging each week.

Then there were the roses. Grampa grew them all together in a large garden, the rows separated by furrows for watering. There were at least three dozen bushes, and they were the centerpiece of the backyard. From the patio, you could count hundreds of flowers when the garden was in full bloom, and it provided a view I never tired of.

Many of the bushes were so well established they towered over me, anchored by roots growing deep into the rich soil. I didn't know how long Grampa had grown roses, yet I knew he was a master. His garden was a never-ending project that evolved slowly over the years, renewing itself each spring with changing colors and scents. He tended his roses with the same love a parent shows a child, and they developed accordingly, blooming with abundance season after season.

Looking back at my childhood, I realize I was being shaped by Grampa as surely as if I was one of his roses. I didn't know that at the time, however; all I knew was I liked to be with him. My regular visits continued as I slowly grew into a young man.

"HOW DO YOU WANT yours done, Scott?" Grampa poked a sizzling steak, then flipped it over.

"Sort of pink inside," I replied.

He nodded and turned another one. "A big teenager like yourself needs a good steak to stay healthy. Which one do you want?"

I pointed at the largest one. "That one. Boy, it smells great."

The tempting aroma of the charcoal barbecue drifted over the patio where the picnic table had been set for a family dinner. As Grampa continued to cook, I looked around the familiar backyard. Many years had passed since my first childhood memories, yet it looked the same as always. My family strolled through the rose garden with Grandma, stopping to smell the different blooms, while I stood on the patio by the barbecue. "You kids are sure growing up fast," Grampa said after turning the meat. "Your brother just graduated and you're not far behind. Seems like only yesterday when you were little."

"Only yesterday?" I replied. "Seems to me like it's taking forever to grow up."

He chuckled. "Don't rush it, Scott. It'll start speeding up soon enough. Before you know what's happening, you'll look back and wonder where the time went."

The evening was cooling off as Grampa put the steaks onto our plates. We sat down to eat, talking about whatever had happened that day, as families always do, laughing between bites of steak, corn-on-the-cob, potato salad, and watermelon. After the dishes were cleared Grampa brought out the ice cream maker and Grandma sliced fresh peaches to top off the dessert. The summer twilight faded slowly, until the last glow of the sunset receded and the time had come to go home.

Grampa was certainly right about one thing: time did begin to pass more quickly the older I got. I graduated from high school a few years after that visit and enrolled at the University of Idaho, several hundred miles from home. For the next four years, I saw Grampa only during holiday breaks and summer vacations. I still treasured the time I spent with him, but before I knew it, college ended and I was setting off to begin life on my own

"THEY'RE BEAUTIFUL."

We had just stepped inside the gate, and Betsy's first words as she saw Grampa's garden expressed her delight. "I've never seen so many roses in one place before."

It was late spring and a lot had happened since the beginning of the year. First had come my commissioning as a lieutenant in the Army, then college graduation, our wedding, and a short honeymoon. Now we were driving across the country to our first duty station in Georgia, passing through town to say good-bye to family and friends. I had brought Betsy to visit my father's parents, and her reaction to the roses reminded me of my mother's first visit to their house many years before. I thought of the story as we walked slowly up and down the rows of my grandfather's garden.

My mother had gone to a country schoolhouse near her farm through the eighth grade, then attended high school in town. There, she met my father and they began to date. Mom always remembered the first time Dad brought her home to meet Grandma and Grampa. She had stepped out of the car in the driveway and simply stopped and stared. Over the gate by the garage grew a breathtaking sight: a huge climbing rose, planted and carefully trained by my grandfather into a perfectly symmetrical green arch. The tall bush was covered with hundreds of red blooms and seemed to burst with brilliant color, standing in sharp contrast to the white house and garage as it bridged the small gap between the two. Out in the country where Mom had been raised they didn't have time for the careful training of climbing roses, and she had never seen anything like it in all her sixteen years. It was a memory she had always treasured.

Betsy pulled a bloom close to smell it. "I've seen roses planted in flower beds or around the edges of lawns, but never so many together in a garden. And the bushes are so gigantic."

"Grampa grows amazing roses," I agreed. "I've never seen nicer ones anywhere."

My new bride slid her arm through mine. "I love it."

We walked back to the house and rang the bell. As we visited with my grandparents, I felt as if I was starting off on something big, and I could tell Grampa understood. He had seen me grow from a child into a young adult, and he knew how important the moment was. He looked me up and down, his eyes speaking volumes but his words simple. "Scott, I want you to know I'm proud of you."

We stood to leave and he reached out to shake hands. As Betsy and I walked out the back door I caught a last glimpse of his rose garden, then we were waving good-bye as we sped on our way.

I HAD EXPECTED the call, yet the words were still hard to believe.

"He died last night, in the hospital in Boise." Mom's voice on the phone seemed faint and far away, filtered by the two thousand miles between us. I felt sad as I looked out our apartment window at the Georgia sunset. The end had come so fast. Barely two months had passed since I looked into his eyes and felt the firm grip of his handshake as I said good-bye. Even then he had felt a bit ill, but he'd thought it was nothing—a few tests, some rest, and he'd be fine.

The doctor had said the brain tumor was too deep. All they could do was wait, try to make him comfortable, and talk. Grandma had stayed close by his side, where she had stood for decades. Family surrounded him, comforting him during his final days.

I couldn't get back for the funeral, so my turn to say good-bye came a few months later when I was home on leave. I found his grave in the small cemetery on the edge of town and looked around uncertainly, not sure what to do. My family had told me about the service, and as I stood in the silence I tried to picture what it must have looked like.

The entire ceremony had been done at graveside, simple and dignified, as Grampa would have wanted. A lifetime of friends had come to pay their respects, standing quietly among the headstones near the surrounding fields. I closed my eyes for a moment and pictured the people saying good-bye, their minds filled with wonderful memories of his life, just as mine was. I could see his dark wooden casket, covered with a tribute to his favorite pastime: dozens upon dozens of red roses arranged in a breathtaking display. I opened my eyes and looked at the single rose engraved on his granite headstone. I smiled as I traced it with my finger, sad he was gone, yet thankful for the years I had known him.

Time moved on and I thought of Grampa a lot as my life unfolded. Within a few years, I had two young children of my own, Robby and Eric. We visited my home town nearly every summer, and I enjoyed watching my boys work around the farm with their own grampa, my dad. I smiled every time they set out with him to take care of some small chore, knowing they were being shaped by him as they grew up just as I had been by my grandfather. They didn't know it, but they were building memories that would last them a lifetime.

GRANDMA GREETED EACH of us with a hug. "It's so good to see you." We were home once again, and I had brought the boys to play for a while at their great-grandmother's house.

Robby and Eric went to the basement and pulled out the Lincoln Logs, just as I had done as a child. *The third generation playing with those same toys*, I thought, smiling as I heard the sounds of a miniature city being constructed on the concrete floor. Grandma and I talked in the living room, then I went down to the basement to check on the boys. They were happily stacking logs.

I wandered around as I always did when I visited, enjoying the memories. I ended up in a small storage room behind the furnace, and without thinking, I pulled open the top drawer of an old dresser. Suddenly, I caught my breath. There was Grampa gazing up at me from an old black and white photograph I had never seen before. I picked up the enlarged photo and studied it closely, lingering over each detail. The image had been captured in the fall, and as usual he was wearing his felt hat. A smile played across his face as he posed for the camera.

"Who's that, Daddy?" Robby was standing at the door of the room.

I turned the picture toward him. "It's your great-grandfather." He looked at me questioningly, so I added, "It's Grampa's dad."

He nodded. "He looks like you."

I turned the photo back and looked at it again. "Yes, he does . . . or I look like him, I guess."

"Did I know him, Daddy?" Robby asked.

"No, Son, you never met him. His name was William, and that's where you got your middle name." I gave a small sigh. "I used to come here and see him a lot, but he's been gone since before you were born."

"Oh." He sounded disappointed.

I looked at the expression on his face. "You want to know what he was like?"

"Sure."

"Well, Rob, let's see." I thought for a moment, memories filling my mind. "He was a bit taller than I am, and he was a very nice man. A hard worker, but he always had time to do things with me because he loved to see his grandchildren." I paused, then added, "You know, you could just think about your own grampa, because he was a lot like him."

He smiled and went back to the log house he was working on. I took a final, long look at the photo. *I wish my boys could have known you, Grampa. You would have loved them . . . as much as I know you loved me.*

I put the picture away, turned off the light, and closed the door of the small room. I walked out to where the boys were playing. *How do you teach a child about someone they never met?* Eric put another Lincoln Log on the cabin he was building, and a thought occurred to me. *It's all in the little things. Small pieces of memories that add up over the years to form a picture they won't be able to forget. Just like my own memories of Grampa.*

I realized one thing more as I stood there with my children. As their father, a lot of the picture they would remember from their youth was up to me. That may seem obvious, yet I had never really considered it before. I nodded slowly. *It's all in the little things.*

"You guys thirsty?" I said. "I bet your great-grandma's got some ginger ale upstairs for us."

OUT IN MY DRIVEWAY, next to the gate at the side of the garage, grows a climbing rose. I planted it a few years ago, the summer after we bought the house. It's not the kind of rose that grows very quickly, and it's only now reaching higher than my head. Yet each year the roots sink a bit deeper, the stems get a bit taller, and every summer it continues to produce dozens of beautiful red blooms.

Sometimes my boys ask to help when they see me taking care of it. I always let them, because each time they trim a thorny branch, or sprinkle fertilizer on the rich soil, I feel they're getting to know my Grampa. They'll never be able to see him in his plaid shirt and felt hat, or feel his hand on their shoulder, or hear his kind voice, yet I believe they are connecting with him in some way, just as I am.

It's hard to say good-bye when somebody you love passes on, but as long as you keep them in your memory they are never completely gone. If their humor, or their character, or even their favorite hobby lives on in your own life, then everyone who knows you also knows them in some small way.

I'm learning a little more about how to grow roses every year, just as I'm slowly getting better at raising my children. I feel fortunate I had my Grampa to give me a good start in both areas, because he showed me the value of patience, tender care, and regular attention when working with something you love. Those qualities always bring out the best in anything you do, and they will cause a child to bloom as surely as they will a rose.

❖   ❖   ❖

RIDING LESSON:

In the garden of life, memories are the rich soil
from which all else grows.

42

All Work and No Play

AHHHHH . . .

This feels good, I thought, *really good.* I turned and felt the sharp streams of water bite into my back, washing the last of the soap suds down the drain. *Now, the soak.* I turned the water temperature up and adjusted the shower head. *Nothing feels better than a long, hot shower in the morning.*

The bathroom door cracked open. "Oh, thank goodness you're alive! I thought maybe you had drowned and left the water running!"

Dang! I had miscalculated again. Rushing through my morning chores, I figured I had a good ten minutes before Dad would come back inside. But his "father sense" must have been set on high that morning, allowing him to detect any water running for more than three minutes.

"If you're going to live in there, I'll rent your room out. Otherwise, you're wasting water. Get out!" The door closed again.

Oh well, I sighed, turning off the shower. *Tomorrow I'll try again. And some day,* I thought, *some day I'll have my own shower . . . and I* will *live in it, if I want to!* That day wasn't to come for many years, because I was only in high school. Until then, I was left with the necessity of using Dad's water, which came from an electric water heater connected somehow to a kilowatt-counter in his brain.

Mentally, I went over Dad's four principles of showering as I dried myself off. First, there was no need for more than one cleaning substance, since a bar of soap could wash hair and body in one application. Second, the water temperature should be kept only one degree above goose bump. Third, after an initial wetting the water should be turned off while soaping occurred, then turned on only briefly to rinse. Finally, and most important: if you felt you were starting to enjoy yourself, it was time to get out immediately.

"But I have hair!" I had protested on more than one occasion, to no avail. Because Dad's follicles had been dormant for many years, he felt unsympathetic to my teenage grooming habits. His water logic always came down to one thing: when you work for it, you can decide how to waste it.

Work, I thought, plugging in the blow dryer. *Everything always comes down to work.*

Like all children, I had started out in life with a natural talent in one particular area, something I could do better than anything else: I could play. Through diligent practice, I had taken my talent to the level of a professional, able to play for hours under any circumstances. If I could have pursued my natural ability, I would have gone through life without a care, yet there existed one big problem: my parents. With no consideration for my feelings on the subject, they decided to make me work.

I was still moaning about the unfairness of it all in my showering years as a teenager. However, my struggles had begun when I was much younger, in grade school, soon after we moved out to our small farm. Without consulting my brother, sister, or me on our schedules, Mom and Dad dictated a list of chores each of us had to do every day.

At my young age I didn't easily submit to such discipline. I still clung to the childish conviction that someone else would do my work if I avoided it long enough. I studied the situation for months as I trudged through my chores, trying to figure a way out of the daily grind of feeding and watering a bunch of ungrateful animals.

One day as I scooped up a bucket of grain to feed the sheep, it hit me: I was alone. My brother and sister had their own chores to do, Dad was working in town, and Mom was in the house. *Ah ha!* I thought to myself, *a loophole! How will anyone know if I do these stupid chores?* For my parents to think I would work on my own, totally unsupervised, amounted to a serious error in judgment on their part. I tossed the bucket back into the grain bin and slammed the door. Since I didn't invent the honor system, I didn't think I should be bound by it.

As I walked by the line of hungry sheep staring expectantly through the fence, I smirked at them. "Sorry girls. I quit."

Within a few short hours, I discovered something quickly learned by every kid who lives on a farm: unfed animals keep no secrets.

I could hear Mom calling down to my basement room from the top of the stairs. *Now what?* I thought. *Why is it so hard to get a minute to myself around this place?* I shuffled out of my room and looked up the stairs at her. "Yes?"

"Are you busy?" She was speaking in a tone of voice that only experienced mothers know how to use, coating her words with a thin frosting of maternal sweetness.

"Well," I replied slowly, trying to read her mood, "I did just start something important."

"That's nice." Her tone sounded worse. "If you don't mind, could you come up here a moment? There's someone who wants to talk to you."

I shrugged and walked up the stairs. "Who's here?" I asked. We lived miles away from any of my acquaintances.

She smiled sweetly. "Oh, a few of your friends are outside."

We stepped out the back door. "I don't see anyone."

Mom guided me around our parked car. "Stand over here and look that way," she said, pointing toward the barnyard. "I think you may have forgotten who your friends are."

I turned the corner and was overwhelmed by a loud chorus of bleating sheep.

There he is! they seemed to be screaming. *Let's get him!* A second-grader isn't much taller than a good-sized sheep, and I began to feel uneasy over their aggressiveness.

"I don't think those are my friends," I said.

All trace of maternal frosting had disappeared, as had her smile. "No kidding. I hope they can control themselves when you carry a bucket of grain into the corral." She turned to go back in the house. "Listen, the sheep eat before you do. That's the way it works on a farm."

Tough love they call it now, but back then it was just tough luck.

Mom and Dad's having informants in the animal world made me feel I couldn't make a move they didn't know about. This feeling alone made me set aside play long enough to finish my assigned work, although I rarely did it willingly. Although I constantly looked for ways to pursue my own agenda, my next big chance at work avoidance didn't come until I left grade school.

My responsibilities had expanded over the years, and the summer after seventh grade I had various jobs to complete in the fields. By that age I was resigned to the reality of Mom finding out if my barnyard chores lapsed, yet I didn't believe her eyesight extended past the sheep corrals.

One day, the early morning sun found me in the far corner of one of our pastures, slowly chopping down thistles with a shovel. The work wasn't exciting, and the hotter the day became, the less excited I felt. After an hour I stopped to wipe the sweat from my forehead. Leaning against the shovel, I surveyed the results of my efforts, and was dismayed that I hadn't yet chopped through a fourth of the thistle patch. The project looked as if it would take the entire day. *Break time,* I thought, sitting down on the bank of a wide ditch that carried irrigation water across the end of the pasture.

I stared at the weeds waving in the warm sun. *What a worthless job. Who's going to know if I finish this anyway?* I looked at our house in the distance, shimmering in the heat, and couldn't see Mom anywhere outside. *I'm out here working my fingers to the bone by myself.*

I tossed a rock into the ditch. The resulting splash looked like a small explosion to my boyish mind, and I picked up a larger rock and threw it in with greater force. *That's cool,* I thought, the weeds already forgotten. *Let's try a handful of rocks.*

If you've never experienced the joy of throwing big rocks into muddy water—or if you've never been a boy—you probably won't understand what came over me. To my youthful eyes, each splash represented much more than the momentary result of a tossed rock; it was the explosion of a falling bomb, a speeding missile, or a massive cannonball. The situation was out of my control, really, since I was simply responding to natural male instinct. At first the splashes were merely innocent amusement, but when a small piece of wood came floating by, the innocent part ended. *Battle stations! Enemy ship approaching!*

Within two minutes, I determined the enemy craft could not be sunk by the small cannonballs lying around the pasture, and I went in search of larger ammunition. The big rocks rested on the opposite bank of the ditch, and I waded across to seize them for the use of my military forces before they fell into enemy hands. Before I knew what was happening, I became completely consumed by the pursuit of the unsinkable piece of wood, criss-crossing the ditch to try different angles of attack and using the shovel to dig up large chunks of sod to heave in. The sun continued to beat down on my bare head. I was soon sweating harder than when chopping weeds, yet like a truly dedicated soldier, I didn't even pause to wipe my brow. After all, this was much more serious than either work or play — it was war.

After an unknown period of time, I watched the wood float around a bend and I turned back to the pasture. *Oh, the weeds.* I had forgotten them in the heat of battle. I shook my head; for some reason I didn't feel rested after my break. I glanced up at the sun overhead. *Oh well, it's lunch time, anyway. Maybe I'll have more energy after I eat.* Laying the shovel across my shoulder, I strolled slowly back to the house.

I left my wet boots on the back step and wandered into the kitchen. "Hi, Mom. What's for lunch?"

She was staring out the kitchen window. "Oh, I haven't thought about lunch yet."

Why not? I thought. *You've got a hungry, weed-choppin' man here!* I had learned respect, however, in word if not in thought, and I knew better than to use a demanding tone of voice with my mother. "Any particular reason?" I said, trying to sound unconcerned.

"I'm enjoying the view out this window. It's amazing how far I can see."

Something told me I was headed into dangerous territory, yet I didn't know how to avoid it. "Oh? I've never noticed."

"Well, come over here and take a look." She motioned me forward, and I stood beside her uncertainly. "See?" she said, pointing. "From this window I can see clear to the mountains up north. And I can see those hills in the distance where they slope up from the desert."

"Yep. Looks real nice," I nodded, growing uneasy.

"I can even see over the sheep corrals and across the pasture to the ditch." I felt her trap closing, and I thought it best not to incriminate myself further by opening my mouth. "What in the world were you doing out there?" she went on. "You've got a whole day's work to take care of and you were wading around in the ditch!"

"Well, I was, uh . . . taking a shortcut."

"A shortcut to where?"

"The other side?" It was the best I could come up with.

She turned back to the window. "You know, I can't concentrate on lunch while my beautiful view of the pasture is blocked."

"Blocked by what?" I said quietly, still hoping to escape punishment.

"By weeds."

I headed back out to the pasture with my shovel, being careful not to sigh until I was out of her hearing. Mom had much sharper eyes than I gave her credit for, and as I chopped my way through the rest of the thistles, I arrived at two conclusions: I would have to work faster when Mom could see me, and I needed to determine which fields were visible from the house as soon as possible.

By the time I hit the showering years in high school, I had finally figured out there was a time for play and a time for work, and mixing them in the proper proportion took good judgment and hard experience. The trick was to make the best possible use of working hours so there would be more time for play, yet that was a concept I had trouble absorbing.

As I finished my sophomore year, my father could tell I was desperately in need of a lesson on the value of time. Dad firmly believed in on-the-job training as the best way to teach children anything, probably because it provided him with so much entertainment.

"You know," he said with a touch of nostalgia as we looked over our one-story barn, "I painted this thing myself when I was about your age." Our farm had been in the family for several decades and my father often recalled the labors of his youth, usually before he made a point for my benefit. He nodded his head. "If my memory serves me right, it only took me about a week or so."

I rolled my eyes behind his back. *Here we go,* I thought. *Another hardship story from the pioneer days.*

"Of course," he went on, "I could only paint at night after spending all day in the fields, and I'm sure I got paid only a dollar or two for the whole project. Back then, kids were happy to earn what they could." He looked at me directly. "So, what do you think would be a fair price today?"

"Uh . . . ten dollars an hour?" I asked hesitantly, not wanting to undervalue my services.

"You're kidding, right?"

"Well, the roof comes to an awfully high peak, you know. Danger costs extra."

He smiled. "I see. I guess you'll have to get your sister to hold the ladder if you feel scared." He set down a can of white paint. "I won't pay you by the hour, Son. Fifty bucks for the whole project — take it or leave it."

Fifty dollars sounded like a small fortune to me, so I knew there had to be a catch. "How soon do I have to finish?" I asked.

Dad handed me a paint brush. "That," he said, turning to walk away, "is entirely up to you."

It seemed too good to be true: paint at my own schedule and receive a big payoff at the end. I couldn't believe I would be able to work as slowly as I wanted in full view of my parents, yet it was fact; they simply sat on the patio and ignored me the first afternoon I went out to scrape off the flaking paint. *This is strange,* I thought. *But if they're not going to get excited, then I won't either. Besides, the sooner I finish, the sooner they'll give me something else to do.* My teenage wisdom told me in this situation, the best approach was to take it easy.

I spent the next month and a half slowly painting my way around the modest-sized barn, working only when the mood struck me. I actually enjoyed myself, and I was happy Dad had finally seen the light and come up with a sensible approach to work. He did keep flashing an amused smile at me whenever I picked up the paint brush, which seemed odd, but parents were prone to unexplainable behavior. When I had slapped the finish coat on the last board and cleaned my brush for the final time, I approached Dad for payment.

"You're done?"

"Done. And with no help from my sister," I said smugly. "That's the most thorough paint job any barn has ever had."

"Well, I can't argue with that, considering you turned a one-week project into a summer work-study program." He put on one of his smirks and pulled out a piece of paper and a pencil.

"Let's see. At your lightning-fast speed, I estimate you spent one hundred and forty hours on the barn. At fifty dollars for the whole project, my calculations show your wage rate to be . . ." He scratched with his pencil. "A bit less than thirty-seven cents an hour."

"And your point?" I asked, feeling I'd walked right into another parental trap.

"Oh, no particular point," he said, handing over two twenties and a ten. "But now that we've established how cheap you'll work, it's time to get started on the next project."

I learned how to put in an honest day's effort that summer, feeling all the while that if I had any rights at all, they were being severely violated. At the time, my father and I had a difference of opinion on what to call hard work done for low pay—I called it forced labor, while Dad used the term "character building."

I held many jobs during high school and college and learned something from each. But the fundamentals of work and play were taught to me on our farm, under the watchful eye of my mother and the patient instruction of my father. By the time I left the farm and headed off on my own, they had taught me there was a time for work and a time for play; each had its place. Finding the proper balance between the two, however, was up to me.

I'd always thought the day I left home I would finally be free to do anything I wanted without answering to anyone. Instead, I discovered I was burdened with a load much heavier than all of my parents' rules put together: the oppressive weight of responsibility.

I married right after college, and as I prepared to enter the Army I realized I had a family to support. As much as I tried to figure a way out, there was only one thing I could do to earn money, and it all came down to my lifelong enemy: work. As I started my first officer training course, I heaved a mental sigh and decided I didn't have much time left for play any more. On the scale of life, play simply didn't tip the balance toward success.

One of the greatest shocks of my life came when I discovered how expensive living on your own can be. Faced with this harsh reality, I threw myself into every job I held in the Army, working at full speed as I attacked my projects and assignments. Laboring for hours at a time without breaks soon became standard, and I wondered if Mom and Dad would recognize me. Was this the same kid they used to drag out of bed each morning, now getting up on his own before 6:00 AM for physical training and not coming home until dinner?

My work habit, so long and slow in growing, soon controlled my daily life, and grew more deeply ingrained with each passing year. By the time I left the military, I held the unshakable belief I could subdue any job in the civilian world if I simply exerted myself hard enough.

As I surveyed the landscape of the business world, I determined my objective would be financial success, and nothing was going to stand in my way. *Heck,* I thought as I started my first office job, *I used to show up for physical training at six in the Army — why not follow the same schedule here?* Success, I figured, would be automatic if I spent that much time at work. I immediately discovered something I could scarcely believe: my long hours weren't enough to accomplish everything. Not only my boss, but the mailbox, telephone, and fax machine issued my marching orders, and I couldn't argue back to any of them. Everything seemed to have a deadline attached — usually a short one.

No job, I vowed, *is going to get the best of me.* I was already putting in long hours, so only one solution remained: work faster. *If I put out more effort, I'm sure I can catch up.*

Nearly every worker in America has found himself or herself in the same vicious circle: the faster I worked, the more I got done; the more I got done, the more I was given to do; the more there was to do, the faster I had to work. The pace never slowed over the next four years, and I found myself thinking constantly of my job, even at home. I began to feel guilty when not sitting at my desk. The military had demanded long hours, but at least they had pinned a couple of medals on my chest for good performance. *This is just as much work as the Army,* I thought as I dragged myself out of bed each morning, *with none of the glory.*

"So, how long have you had high blood pressure?" The doctor stared at me intently, waiting for an answer.

I wasn't sure what to say. "No one has ever told me my blood pressure was high," I finally replied, understanding why the nurse had acted so concerned as she scribbled on my chart.

"Well," he said, "I'm telling you now. What's going on in your life?"

The question was too big for me to answer on short notice, so I told him what was going on that day. I had torn myself away from work for a routine physical examination and I was anxious to return to my desk; files were stacked high and messages were waiting to be returned. I tried for a few minutes to convince the doctor of the importance of my hurried pace, but he wasn't impressed.

"Well, all I can say is that you're killing yourself." He handed me a small card. "Carry this in your wallet so you can keep a record of your blood pressure readings. You need to stop by the office once a week to check it." He turned to go. "Could be time for a few changes."

As I sat in the parking lot outside the doctor's office I looked at the card. *What has happened to me?* Without realizing it, I had become obsessed with work. I sighed and shook my head as I started the car and headed back to the office. I couldn't even remember what had been so important when I left. *It is time for me to get a life.*

But how? I knew I needed to play more, to relax, yet there seemed no end to the work, even at home. Each weekend I made a long list of projects, and I didn't stop until I had crossed the last one off. Unfortunately, when you've spent several years coiling yourself into a tight ball of anxiety, it is difficult to unwind. *How am I supposed to relax when I have so much to do?*

I was still thinking about it the next day as I stepped into my morning shower. I soaped myself up, working methodically and quickly out of habit. As usual, my mind was already preoccupied with the tasks facing me at work. As the last of the suds swirled down the drain, I reached to turn off the water, then stopped with my hand on the knob. *Boy, this sure feels good.* I straightened up and turned my back to the stream of hot water. *Maybe just a little soak.*

For years, I had automatically limited my use of hot water when I showered. Yet as I soaked with abandon, it dawned on me that I owned an inexpensive gas-fired water heater with a fifty-gallon tank. And I got up before anyone else in the family. *And who is going to stop me from draining the tank if I feel like it?*

The next day I took a cup of coffee into the shower with me, just because I could. Within a couple of weeks, I bought a no-fog mirror, stuck it to the wall, and started shaving in there. *Hey, Dad!* I thought, smiling triumphantly through the rising steam, *Look at me! I'm not dead and the water is still running! Yes, Dad, I am living in the shower!*

It felt as good as I remembered, and it was the beginning of a very long unwinding process. As with all change, learning to relax is difficult and takes time. I've made a lot of progress, but it's something I'm still working on, one day at a time.

I'm careful, though, since it wouldn't be right for the kids to see me enjoying myself too much. In their eyes, I am a tireless worker, setting the example all day long with my labors. I know their little characters need building, and the seed of a work habit must be planted when they are young or it may never take root. Of course, they play a lot—much more than I did back in the old days, I'm sure. And that's good, because they'll need to remember how to goof off when they start searching for their own balance in life.

Maybe one day they'll call me for advice. They'll be stressed out by work, perhaps, wondering how to back off and take it easy. There's a good chance I won't be available, though, because by that time I'll once again be playing like a professional, as I was in my childhood. Professionals, you see, don't allow distractions when practicing their art. The kids can leave a message, because there'll be plenty of time to call them back.

Just as soon as I get out of the shower.

❖　　　❖　　　❖

RIDING LESSON:

To put your job in perspective, try describing the details of your daily work to your kids and see how long it takes their eyes to glaze over.

THE HEART
GROWS FONDER

MOM REACHED UNDER the tree and pulled a piece of crumpled wrapping paper and a curled length of green ribbon out of the way. She peered behind the folds of the tree skirt, then announced, "There's one left, back in the corner." Smiling, she glanced over to where I was sitting amongst the gifts from my fifth Christmas. "The last present of the day."

She reached in and brought out a small package, about the size of a deck of cards, carefully wrapped in red paper with a golden tag taped to the top. Mom lifted the tag and read, "To Anne, from Scott." She held out the present in my direction. "I wonder what it could be?"

Mom knew exactly what I had purchased, since she had watched while I picked the gift out at the store. But she was enjoying the moment, knowing it could be one of those times a parent doesn't often see. "Go on, give it to her."

My sister stood up from her other presents and turned to look at me. She was four, one year younger than I, and we were wearing home-made flannel pajamas cut from the same cloth. Her hair was held back by a small clip, revealing large brown eyes that matched mine. She held her hands together and looked at me expectantly, not saying a word.

Suddenly, I felt very uncomfortable. I took the package from Mom, walked to Anne and thrust it toward her without ceremony. "Here."

I stood close by as she meticulously began unwrapping the small box, watching her face for any reaction. Anne had no reason to expect anything nice from me, since I was rarely pleasant to her. In fact, I hadn't intended to buy this particular gift when I'd headed out to the store with my mother; if given the chance, I would have preferred to skip my sister's present entirely. But I had seen it under the glass counter of the dime store and decided without hesitation. For some reason, in spite of my normal aversion to being nice to my sister, I had known it would be perfect. Mom, surprised at my choice, had been happy to buy the gift for a few dollars and had helped me wrap it up and letter the tag.

Anne tore the last of the paper off and held the small, white box up for closer examination. After one more solemn glance at me, she carefully removed the lid and took out a layer of cotton. Her eyes widened and her lips lifted in the beginnings of a smile. Reaching into the box, she pulled out a pin the size of a half-dollar and held it up.

"It's a butterfly!" She admired the pink, orange, and white pin for a long moment, her eyes shining. "Put it on, please, Mommy!" In spite of myself, I felt good inside and couldn't help smiling as I watched my sister's excitement. Anne turned to me, the pin glowing from her pajamas, and hesitated.

"Thank you." Another moment of hesitation, then a hug, a small one, over before I could react in my usual manner of distaste.

"Uh, you're welcome," I mumbled as I shuffled back to my own pile of presents. *She didn't have to go and hug me!* I thought. *It's going to take all day to make her mad at me again!*

My sister. Why did those two words bring out such a mean streak in me? As far back as I can remember, Anne never acted in a way deserving of retaliation. She certainly never did anything to compare with the treatment I got from my brother, two and a half years older than me. If I ever needed a reason to be mean to a person, he provided one at an early age.

"Hold it steady," Brett had said, raising his makeshift bow and arrow to shoulder height. "Come on, it's not that heavy. Quit wobbling!"

"I'm trying!" At age four, I was shorter than the Hula Hoop that Brett had instructed me to hold out at arm's length. I didn't want to disappoint him, so I struggled to keep it up. At my young age I had a poorly developed sense of danger, so I didn't even flinch as I faced a drawn bow only eight feet from my face. After all, he was older and must know what he was doing, right?

"Hold still. I'm going to shoot it right through." Brett had spent a full morning making the bow from a couple feet of white string and a stick he'd found in the back yard. The arrow was another stick, sharpened by rubbing on the sidewalk. No feathers, only a small split in one end to form a notch for the bow string. He strained to pull back on the end of the arrow and squinted, carefully aiming at the large circle only a few steps away from him. He was standing so close, how could he miss?

Twang! The arrow sliced through the air and found its mark: my right eye. Fortunately, a sidewalk-sharpened arrow is not the most deadly of projectiles and my vision survived. I didn't hold his actions against him; the whole incident never upset my childhood respect for my older brother, in spite of the black eye. I probably would have been stupid enough to hold the hoop again if he had told me to.

Although Anne never jabbed me in the eye with a stick, I treated her as if she had done much worse. Perhaps we were simply too close in age to get along, but more likely, I was just plain mean at that age. Whatever the reason, I didn't know how to be nice to her for more than five minutes at a time. But who could blame me? I mean, she was my *sister*. I wasn't alone, however; I had plenty of assistance from Brett in making her life miserable.

"Okay, we'll say it again." Brett winked at me. We were practicing our favorite pastime of driving Anne crazy, this time by excluding her from the family. "We'll name all the kids, including the cousins. Listen carefully."

Smirking, we started down the list together. "Brett, Scott, *and* Carrie, Patrick, Julie, Patty, Susan."

"You did it again! You said *'and,'* not *'Anne!'*"

"We said it. You just weren't listening closely. We'll start over . . ." It's not hard to see why parents are so fond of repeating the phrase "if you can't say anything nice, don't say anything at all." Children's tongues have the capacity to be so sweet, yet they can also cause much pain, especially to siblings.

I was decent to Anne when it suited my purposes, such as when I needed a playmate, but only when we were alone. I definitely didn't want to be closely associated with her in public, lest my friends think poorly of me. This ruled out sitting next to her on the school bus, or speaking to her at recess. Ignoring her became a habit, one that became more and more common the older I got.

My memories of Anne start to fade out at about the time I entered high school. I know she was there at the same time, but I was more concerned about my hair than about my own sister or anything she was doing. If you had asked me about her, I wouldn't have been able to say, with much accuracy, what was going on in her life. She was my kid sister; what else was there to talk about? But she wasn't a kid any more, and if I had been paying attention I would have seen she was growing up fast. And changing, like me.

As I had followed my brother to college at the University of Idaho, Anne followed me. My ignoring her continued, but I took it to a new level. Although we lived on different floors of the same dorm complex, I took pride in not visiting her room a single time during my entire sophomore year. Why? I can't honestly say now, yet it gave me great satisfaction at the time. I even bragged to my friends about it.

The time at college was the last we lived in the same building. The years of childhood are so quickly over, and before I knew it they were gone. Anne faded further from my mind as I began to struggle up the steep learning curve of young adulthood. Trying to figure out married life, kids, and the Army took all my time and left no mental space for my sister. Strangely enough, when the connection between us had stretched so thin it could have broken altogether, I gradually began building a new relationship with my closest sibling. Distance, like a view from a mountain top, often gives us a perspective we cannot achieve when we are too close to the details. It was a slow process, but over the years we began to find some common ground.

"How did Dad's visit go last weekend?" I was talking to Anne on the phone, sprawled on the sofa one evening after my kids were in bed.

I could hear her laugh echoing around her small apartment. "Dad acted more practical than ever. He was dying to do some projects. He had the refrigerator pulled out and was vacuuming off the coils within twenty minutes of walking in the door. 'Makes the motor work too hard if there's not proper ventilation,' he kept saying."

"Boy, I wish he'd come visit me," I replied. "I can't seem to remember those lessons he used to teach on changing faucet washers. Now I have dripping faucets, and I wish I'd paid attention."

Anne laughed again. "Just make sure your furnace filter isn't dirty if he decides to come visit. That sin is unforgivable."

"Yeah, I can imagine," I chuckled. "I miss him and Mom. Time goes by so fast and before you know it, a year has passed since you've seen them."

"Yeah, I know," said Anne. "I miss them, too."

Hanging up the phone after such conversations, I had to admit I didn't miss only my parents, but Anne as well. I felt surprised by this at first. The more I considered it, though, the more I realized I had spent much of my life with my sister. I recalled that my earliest memory involved Anne. Whether the memory was real or merely the result of seeing a picture in the family photo album, I had always called it my first.

In the black and white image in my mind, Anne and I are crouching in small rubber boots side by side at the end of our driveway. Behind us stands a brick house rented by my family in Boise; in front of us is a mud puddle. We are stirring it with our fingers, staring together as we try to see through the murky water to inspect the small wonders of life.

Years later, no longer side by side yet still connected, we were both trying to see our way through adult life, stirring the cloudy water of daily existence to discern the meaning of the changes we were experiencing. The phone calls and visits provided the first realization that I had a lot more in common with my sister than with most other people, and maybe that could be the basis for a friendship.

Maybe. But friendship takes work, especially when you have a long history with someone. It's similar to cleaning out the attic — you have to shove a lot of baggage out of the way before you can even get through the door. Anne was becoming a different person, and before I could call her a friend, I had to acknowledge she wasn't the same sister I used to share a house with. Though our past connected us, it was the one thing standing in the way of our future.

Growing closer to our families as adults, whether it is to our parents or our siblings, can be a difficult process of pulling closer and letting go at the same time. If we truly want to have a relationship, we have to make the effort to stay close, to "pull" toward each other. At the same time we have to let go of the impressions we formed of the person as we were growing up. If a family cannot let the past go, they will never truly be friends with each other.

My increasing years have made me realize how sad it is to always think of family members in the role they played for a few short years in their youth, never accepting that they change, especially after they leave home. That's like saying we stop growing at age eighteen, when our own experience tells us that's when the big lessons are first starting, the lessons that truly shape our lives and our characters.

In the end, it comes down to this: accepting faults and flaws and looking for the good in each other. We must remember the past, yet understand we may have to let parts of it go. Shared memories bind a family together, but if some of them are keeping its members from moving on and becoming friends, it's time to quit dragging them out.

Anne and I were both headed somewhere in life, both searching for the same things. It was time to reach out a hand to help each other along the way.

We kept talking on the phone, and visiting.

"But I don't want her to go!" Robby wiped a tear off his cheek, and another one rolled down to take its place.

"We'll see Aunt Anne at the wedding in a few months," my wife said, giving him a squeeze. "She has to go home now. Go give her a hug. You too, Eric."

"Aunt Anne." That was a role I had never imagined my sister playing when we were growing up. I hadn't imagined her in most of the roles she was coming to play in my life: aunt to my children, confidante to my wife, friend to me. She came to visit often, and the kids always hated to see her leave. We all did. It had been hard over the years to see her returning to her home in another city, alone. Betsy and I had hoped Anne would find someone to share her life with, and now she had, in her own time and not until the right person came along.

"We're all going to see her get married." Betsy smiled at Anne. "And then you'll have a new uncle, too. Uncle Mike."

Anne returned the smile. We were still brother and sister, yet we weren't children any more. I cared about her life, about her happiness, and I felt glad to share in the joy she was finding as she searched out the path to her own dreams.

"We're excited for you." I helped her put her bags into the car. "Let us know if you need any last-minute help when we arrive."

The wedding was classic, small and intimate, arranged completely by my sister. The affair was simple, reflecting the understated, refined sense of style Anne had developed over the years. From the doorway, I could see the entire wedding party and the guests. There were four generations of my family in one room; Great-Grandma Loys, my dad's mother, sat with Robby and Eric, who were most interested in the flower-strewn cake rising in three layers on a table by the fireplace. Many of Anne's friends from work, college, and high school had also come, filling the room with laughter and conversation. I stood with Mom near the guest book.

"This is perfect, isn't it?" she said.

"Yes," I agreed. "Anne really put this together well." I looked around the ballroom of the old mansion. "It's nice to have the family together in one spot."

We had all changed. Mom and Dad weren't the same people as when I had left home fifteen years before, and I knew my life hadn't stood still either. Yet my family had made an effort to keep up with each other. We had made a lot of phone calls, written a lot of letters, and done a lot of talking as our lives unfolded in different directions over the years.

From her position near the punch bowl, Betsy waved to me over the crowd. "It's time to give the toasts," I said to Mom, and began working my way to the front of the room.

Betsy struck a fork against a glass, and the conversation slowly quieted. All eyes were on the bride, standing tall and beautiful in white next to her new husband. Light streaming through the tall windows washed across the crisp linen tablecloths, glinting off sparkling glasses of champagne raised to the happy couple.

Is this my sister? I thought. *She's all grown up. The center of attention with a room full of friends wishing her the best.* Anne had come as far as I had, in her own way.

My turn came. I stepped forward and told a brief story of growing up, of finding your path and following it, of walking with a partner toward your dreams. I held the crowd's attention for only a moment, then all eyes were back on Anne and Mike as I returned to my seat.

The cake was cut and passed out; my kids quickly devoured their pieces and ran off to explore. "You told a nice story," said one guest as she walked by me to get more punch.

"Thanks." *But the real story,* I thought as I finished my cake and followed the children outside, *started a long time ago.*

I stood outside the large double doors and looked for Robby and Eric. Rhododendrons rose to the porch rail, forming a deep thicket of branches. I heard small voices from inside the broad leaves and leaned over to listen.

"It's a moff!" Eric was still working on his "th" sounds. I could see him reaching to touch a small flutter of white wings perched on Robby's finger.

"Don't touch it!" Robby warned. "Just look. It's a butterfly, I think, not a moth. See? It has some orange on its wings." The small creature sat motionless for a long moment as the boys studied it. Eric loved butterflies and I could tell by the expression on his face he was longing to hold it.

Robby held his hand out to him. "Here. Let it crawl to you." With a little prodding, the butterfly worked its way onto Eric's outstretched finger. He beamed as he held it up for closer inspection.

"Thank you, Wobby." Heartfelt and simple. Eric lifted his hand toward a break in the leaves and the butterfly leaped into the air and fluttered away. Then the boys were gone, racing deeper into the jungle along the porch.

Only a moment, frozen in time, I thought. Yet perhaps it would be remembered somewhere deep inside their minds like the butterfly pin I had once given Anne; a small seed, planted young and nurtured by love, that would grow into a relationship as they got older. It would take a lot of work from both of them to stay close over the years. *I hope they want it. If they do, they can have a relationship like Anne and I have developed over time. Maybe, with effort, they will grow closer as they grow up.*

I could hear them calling to each other as they found their way through the darkness beneath the branches. *Maybe, with love, there will come a day when they won't just call each other brother.*

They will call each other friend.

❖　　　❖　　　❖

RIDING LESSON:

As we grow older, we often seek a brotherhood with our friends, but don't seek a friendship with our brother.

Hunting Lessons

THE DAYS WERE GROWING shorter and colder, and the harvest had already begun. As the grain was cut and the hay laid out to dry on our farm, I began to notice them: pheasants, scurrying across open areas, dodging behind clumps of grass, and diving into overgrown ditch banks for cover. We had quite a flock of them prowling around the property, I realized. As I counted them one day during my sophomore year in high school, a strange and unfamiliar feeling began to grow inside me. I had no explanation for it, but for some reason I had the sudden and intense desire to go hunting.

I had never displayed a trace of natural desire toward the sport of hunting. I did have hazy memories of accompanying my dad when I was a child, happy to carry the pheasants he shot and enjoying the sight of our dog working the birds into the open. That had been many years before, however, and hunting as a sport had faded on the Weigle farm; Dad's work at the lumberyard had kept him busy in the fall, and Ginger, the reliable bird dog, was gone. The shotguns had remained undisturbed in the laundry room closet for a long time.

So my current and growing fascination must have come from a different source than my childhood. Perhaps it was a sudden primal urge to fill the pantry for winter, or peer pressure from my hunting friends in high school, or a hormonally induced, temporary obsession with masculine pursuits. Whatever the reason, as I sniffed the smells of the harvest in the crisp fall air, an idea began to form. Following my impulse, I went to take a peek at the shotguns, a new self-image forming in my mind: Scott the Hunter. I realized I would need a little assistance to work out the details of the sport, so I approached my father.

"Hey, Dad, why don't we go out and knock down a few pheasants this weekend?"

He looked at me with surprise. "Hunting? *You* want to go hunting?"

"Well, yes," I replied with a slight pout, my feelings a bit hurt by his obvious show of disbelief. *Just because I couldn't have cared less about hunting for the last sixteen years doesn't mean you have to act so shocked,* I thought.

"I figured maybe we could, you know, set out the decoys and blow on that honker thing you have," I continued, trying to sound nonchalant. "It might be some fun."

"Uh, we don't generally use decoys for pheasants. That's a duck thing, and pheasants don't honk—although they could, I suppose, given the right conditions." Dad paused. "Any particular reason why you suddenly want to go hunting after all these years?"

"No ... I just ... I mean, the timing is right. I think my reflexes have matured enough to handle a shotgun the right way. I wasn't ready before." *And, I have a strong desire to blast something,* I added silently.

"Well, you get yourself a hunting license and we'll see if we can't scare up a couple of pheasants." He turned away, trying to hide a grin.

I got my license the next day and started to prepare for our weekend expedition. My sister walked up as I was pushing shotgun shells through the elastic loops of a hunting vest.

"What are you doing?"

"What does it look like I'm doing? Getting ready to go pheasant hunting with Dad." *Girls! Always full of dumb questions.*

"You don't need to get snotty. I mean, you're not exactly a hunter, you know. Remember the rockchucks?" Anne's lips curled into the beginning of a smirk. "I'm sure the rockchucks remember you!"

I had been afraid someone would bring up the rockchuck incident. It had not been my proudest moment. Rockchucks, called "marmots" by more sophisticated city people who treasure a glimpse of one in a municipal park, are not highly regarded in agricultural circles. They live, as their name implies, in rocky areas. They could grow as big as a small dog, and they have very healthy appetites. We had a rock pile in one of our hay fields that contained a medium-sized herd of the little beasts, and each day they would venture forth and graze the alfalfa down like a band of miniature, buck-toothed, brown cows.

One summer evening a couple of years earlier, my older brother and I had announced we were going to rid the hay field of rockchucks once and for all. We set out with a couple of .22 rifles and a box of ammunition. Mom, Dad, and Anne smiled with amusement, poured glasses of iced tea, and got comfortable in lawn chairs on the back patio to listen to the show. Brett and I traipsed up over the hill, along the small canal, and approached the hay field through the pasture, out of sight of the house and the rockchuck colony. Although we were both short on hunting experience, we instinctively knew we had to stalk our prey to avoid spooking them. Creeping up over a small rise, we parted the tall grass and saw our intended targets basking in the setting sun.

Poor things don't know what's coming, I thought. They were about thirty yards away, hanging out on the rocks, feeling sluggish with their bellies full of alfalfa. *They don't stand a chance.* Brett and I discussed our strategy in whispers. With the semi-automatic rifle, he would lay down a hail of bullets, blanketing the rocks with a shower of flying lead to catch the five or six closest rockchucks before they could roll into their burrows. Like a precision sniper, I would use the single-shot .22 to pick off the ones running in from the field for cover.

"Ready?" he whispered.

"Ready!"

"Aim!"

"Aimed!"

"FIRE!"

Back at the house they heard a sudden, rippling explosion of gunfire, and a small cloud of dust rose up in the direction of the hay field. The dust quickly obscured our vision, but we kept firing at anything that looked suspicious, using up half the box of ammo. After a couple of minutes, Brett said, "Let's let the dust settle so we can count the ones who didn't make it."

As the air cleared, we saw at least a dozen rockchucks in and around the target area, motionless. "Oh my gosh!" I crowed, "We got 'em!" I looked closer. "But . . . they're starting to move." Indeed they were, and not in the manner of wounded animals. They calmly returned to their basking and grazing, apparently unconcerned about what appeared to have been a sudden and brief hailstorm. We hadn't hit a single one of them.

"Maybe our sights are off," Brett suggested. We twiddled around with them, reloaded, and switched guns for good measure. This time we decided to aim each bullet with precision, and began plinking our way through the rest of the ammo, taking care to have a rockchuck directly in our sights before squeezing the trigger.

"Is your gun working?" I asked when we were nearly out of ammo. "I can't get mine to shoot straight." The rockchucks had finally started to amble slowly back to their burrows to prepare for bed, apparently oblivious to the small spurts of dust rising up in random patterns around them.

"Well, mine seems to be working all right," Brett replied, "but maybe it's adjusted for a left-eyed person, and I think I must be right-eyed." He squeezed off the last bullet as the final rockchuck paused at the lip of the burrow and made what appeared to be a rude gesture in our general direction before disappearing from sight. Walking home, we could see our family still sitting on the patio, their smiles evident at a distance.

"How was the war?" Dad asked as we sauntered up nonchalantly. "It sounded like there were at least a dozen rifles going. Were the rockchucks armed and fighting back?"

"I don't see any pelts," smiled my sister.

"Well, there must have been a ton of wounded ones," said Brett. "We thought it would be best to not finish them off so they would be living reminders to the rest that they shouldn't mess with the hay."

"Wounded?" asked Mom. "How could you tell?"

"They seemed to be limping when they crawled back to their holes," I stated matter-of-factly. "They were moving so slowly they must have really been shot up."

Anne started to giggle, and Mom and Dad joined in.

"Well, at least we scared the daylights out of them. They'll certainly think twice before nibbling the alfalfa again!"

So, I had an unfortunate episode of bad luck from my past to overcome, yet that made me more determined to triumph over the pheasants. Bird hunting, in my mind, was much more glamorous than rockchuck hunting, and besides, how could I miss with a shotgun?

Dad didn't take a gun, figuring he needed to keep all his attention on his nervous student to avoid personal injury. I loaded up my 16-gauge once we got clear of the farmyard, and Dad outlined our strategy. We would simply walk the ditch banks to scare up any game hiding in the grass and weeds, making a large circle around our farm through the known pheasant gathering spots. We started out, my finger trembling on the red safety button as I anxiously watched for signs of scurrying birds. We moved along the end of one field, then a second and on across a third.

Must not be any out today, I thought, relaxing my grip on the stock a bit. *Oh well, sometimes the luck isn't with you.* We turned a corner, and suddenly the grass exploded at my feet. A huge rooster pheasant roared into the clear blue sky like a small helicopter taking off, curving away in a smooth arc to my left.

"Do you think you might shoot at it?" Dad asked after a few seconds of inaction.

"Uh . . . ." was all I could manage with my heart in my throat. Forcing myself to breathe, I brought the shotgun up to my shoulder with shaking hands and squeezed off a shot. The pheasant didn't pause.

"I think you need to be a bit quicker on the draw," advised Dad.

I nodded and took a few deep breaths to calm down. *Steady, Scott, steady. You'll get one.* We continued across the next field.

"There's one coming from your left," Dad pointed out a few minutes later. Sure enough, a rooster pheasant was cutting a straight line across my front, his wings held steady in a long, smooth glide. He looked identical to the first one. Not wanting to be accused of slow reflexes again, I whipped the shotgun up to my shoulder and fired in the general direction of the bird. He didn't ruffle a feather as he sailed off to the right behind a clump of trees.

"I generally recommend aiming," said Dad. "It usually produces the best results in this sort of situation."

We had taken only a few more steps when a bird came from my right, darting from the same trees the last one had disappeared behind. My hasty shot missed again, and I watched the pheasant fade into the distance. "Is that the same bird?" I asked Dad as a whiff of smoke curled up from the shotgun. "I'd swear he's messing with me."

"Well, that would be unlikely," he answered. "But not unheard of, I suppose, given the fact that experience tells them when there's nothing to be afraid of." I glared at him, but he just smiled back. "Let's head toward home. I think we need to regroup and plan out a new strategy."

As I unloaded the gun by the cow shed, it occurred to me that hunting may not be as simple as I had imagined, even with a shotgun. As I ejected the last shell and turned toward the house, I caught sight of a pheasant—maybe *the* pheasant—peering at me from behind a clump of weeds. *See ya later*, he seemed to be saying. *Come back and play again!*

Anne was sitting on the back steps when we walked up. I dropped my hunting jacket next to her and she made a big show of searching for pheasants in the game pocket. "Guess I should tell Mom to turn the oven off," she smirked. "No drumsticks for the family table tonight." She snickered at her own cleverness, then asked, "Do you remember what happened last spring?" I shook my head, wishing she would let me mope in peace. "Sure you do: Fritz caught a pheasant. A big one, too."

I remembered. Fritz was our family cat, pure black from nose to tail, and last spring he had actually tackled a pheasant in the pasture next to the house. After spending an hour sneaking up on it, he had pounced on the unsuspecting bird from behind and wrestled it to the ground. The attack made a huge ruckus since the pheasant was bigger than the cat, and the two of them rolled around in a regular barnyard brawl. Although Fritz had required our assistance to subdue his catch, he had strutted around like a proud panther for a week afterward.

My sister went on. "Let me see. Isn't that officially one more than you've ever gotten?"

"Yeah, well . . . ." I stammered, trying to think fast. "His was out of season, and poaching is against the law."

Anne's laughter was a fitting end to my first hunting expedition. I wasn't through yet, though; both my desire and Dad's patience were still holding, so our adventure continued the following weekend.

"Okay, here's the game plan," Dad said as we loaded up again. "Maybe the problem has been walking *and* talking while we hunt, so we need to eliminate the distractions." The advice sounded suspiciously like a comment on my lack of coordination, but I was willing to try anything.

He continued. "So today we'll work the cornfield. I'll walk up from one end and you'll sit at the other end and wait for the birds to fly over; that way you can totally concentrate on aiming." He paused, then added, "And maybe you should spit your gum out."

To put the pheasants at maximum disadvantage, he posted me at the high end of the long, narrow field, up on a small rise that provided a clear view over the top of the corn. He went down to the bottom and began to walk slowly up the rows toward me, making noise to scare the feeding pheasants.

Okay, I thought, *this is it. Stay calm, Scott. Steady on the trigger.* I made sure I had filled my pump-action shotgun with the maximum number of shells, and I forced myself to take several deep breaths. I could see Dad making his way toward me at the other end of the field, his progress marked by waving stalks of corn.

As he neared the half-way point, a sudden rustling occurred. An entire squadron of pheasants, twenty or more, rose up from the field and began to circle, getting into formation like a fleet of bombers preparing to make a run over enemy territory. *Maybe they'll go the other way,* I thought hopefully, starting to lose my nerve as I raised the shotgun to my shoulder. *No, here they come – right toward me!* They were picking up speed, accelerating in a flurry of flapping wings, flying only ten feet above the corn tassels.

Steady, Scott, steady! Hold your fire until you see the whites of their eyes. I wasn't exactly certain pheasants had white eyes, but it did seem best to wait until the birds were almost overhead. A few seconds passed, and they drew closer to my position. I raised the barrel of my shotgun toward the front of the formation and clicked off the safety.

Now! I couldn't wait any longer. *Fire!* The first shot rang in my ears. *Pump in a new shell! Fire! Pump! Fire! Pump!* Adrenaline surged through my veins, and it took several seconds for me to realize that in spite of my frantic activity, I had heard only one shot. As I was beginning to think there must be something wrong with my gun, my feet started to slip and I glanced down. I was standing on a small pile of shells that were still loaded with shot and ready to go. Somehow, I had gotten my *pumps* out of sync with my *fires* and had managed to eject my ammunition unspent.

Hands quivering, sweat dripping off my forehead, I scrambled to load handfuls of dirt and shells back into the gun. My warning shot had not deterred the pheasants from their steady advance; as I jammed in the last of the shells, the lead bird passed over my head, seemingly close enough to touch. *All right, Scott, let's give it to them!* Aiming seemed like a total waste of time. Holding the barrel vertically, I squeezed the trigger and pumped the gun over and over until it stopped producing.

Shortly after, Dad strolled casually up out of the field. "Are we eating pheasant tonight?" One look at the scene answered his question. I sat, sweating, on top of a pile of dirt, surrounded by the remains of a fiercely fought battle: a handful of empty shells, the acrid smell of burnt gunpowder, and slowly settling dust. But no pheasants. Not one. Not even a single feather to show for my efforts.

"Well, maybe we can shoot a couple hamburgers when we get home," Dad smiled. "I wasn't in the mood for bird anyway."

As expected, Anne was waiting when we got back to the house. She had been observing the spectacle from a distance. "Where do you think the pheasants landed after they flew over you?" she asked innocently as I slowly put away my hunting gear.

"I don't know." I could tell she was heading somewhere I didn't want her to go.

"I'll bet they landed in the hay field, right on top of the rock pile." Her little smirk began to grow again. "Probably talking to the rockchucks right now, telling war stories." More smirking.

"Very funny. Go away."

The first snows of winter soon covered the fields, and my primal hunting urge fell dormant, never to fully awaken again. Our farm became a virtual pheasant preserve; hunters in trucks would pause on the road by our fields, staring longingly at the dozens of birds strolling calmly about in the open, unconcerned about any danger from humans.

My hunting instincts, such as they were, did revive for a very brief period in college, where I put them to use in the pursuit of my wife. The relationship progressed to the point where I felt a distinct need to impress her, and the first summer I brought Betsy home to meet the family I casually suggested a little target practice. There's nothing like the smell of gunpowder to win over a woman, or so I had heard. I figured my gun-handling abilities would be adequate enough to impress a city girl, and perhaps even teach her a thing or two about sharpshooting.

We took Dad's .22 pistol out behind the chicken house and arranged a dozen soda cans on the haystack. My student seemed uncertain, but willing, and the marksmanship lesson began.

"Now," I said, speaking as if I knew what I was talking about, "the key to hitting the target is to remain steady, so you'll want to take your time, hold your breath, and squeeze off each shot slowly." I picked up the pistol. "I'll show you."

I loaded six rounds into the revolver. "I personally recommend the two-handed grip on the pistol, because it gives you the best control. With this grip you stand so you are facing the target, but you must remember to close one eye, or at least squint it down real tight." Betsy remained silent. *She must be impressed with my knowledge,* I thought.

I was determined not to repeat the pheasant-hunting mistake of whipping off shots without aiming. I faced the haystack, lifted the pistol to shoulder level, and found a can in my sights. It looked tiny, no matter which eye I squinted, and I found myself wishing I had a shotgun. Holding my breath, I carefully squeezed off a shot.

"I don't think you hit anything," said Betsy.

No kidding, I thought. I sucked in another breath and held it, then shot at the same can five more times. It didn't budge. Turning slightly red, I reloaded and handed the pistol to Betsy. "Here. You try. I've, uh, warmed up the gun for you."

Betsy took up a stance with the two-handed grip I had demonstrated and squeezed off a careful shot. Nothing. "Are you sure this is the way to do it?"

"Do what?" asked a voice from behind us.

I turned around. Mom had walked up to observe our marksmanship class. "We're shooting cans," I explained, "and I'm giving Betsy a lesson. Do you want to give it a try?"

"Oh, sure. Why not?" Mom held out her hand, and Betsy handed over the pistol. *Maybe Mom will be a better student,* I thought as I began the instruction over. *I'll prove I can teach at least one woman to shoot.*

"Now, Mom, you're going to want to hold that gun with two hands and face the target squarely." I demonstrated, gripping my palms together and extending my index finger out like the barrel of a gun. "Close one eye and slowly squeeze off a shot to avoid jerking around." I squinted one eye down and mimicked firing a shot. Holding my pose to demonstrate follow-through, I muttered out the side of my mouth, "Any questions?"

Pow!

I jumped in surprise as a soda can spun through the air. I looked at Mom and my jaw dropped in amazement. She was standing sideways to the targets, holding the pistol only in her right hand with her arm extended out straight at shoulder level. With barely a pause, she shifted her aim and pulled the trigger again, sending another can flying. She emptied the revolver in a few seconds, each shot finding its mark.

Mom lowered the smoking gun. "What were you saying? I didn't hear all of it."

As I searched for words, Betsy, a sly grin growing on her face, interjected, "I think he was about to say a boy should always listen to his mother." I couldn't argue with that piece of wisdom, especially since the mother we were discussing was armed. The lesson ended, and we walked back to the house to put the gun away. Anne was sitting on the patio, having seen the whole thing.

Oh, great, I thought. *Here we go again.*

She didn't bother to comment directly on my marksmanship. Instead, she nonchalantly asked, "Guess what happened last month while you were away at college, Scott?" She paused a moment, not for an answer but for dramatic effect. "Fritz caught another pheasant. Sneaked right up and jumped on it." She smirked a little. "I checked, and he wasn't armed. Must have been working on pure hunting instinct. You know, the kind available to *normal* males."

Betsy was smiling.

"And your point?" I asked.

"Oh, I'm not trying to make any point. I just thought you'd want to know Fritz has now bagged two pheasants. I'm not keeping score or anything, but I believe his lifetime total would now be, let's see . . ." She made a big show of counting her fingers. "Exactly two more than you. Right?"

Female laughter can be a wonderful sound in most circumstances. If you're a man and you're outnumbered, however, the sound of laughter is probably coming at your expense. I left to put the pistol away so I wouldn't spoil their fun.

The Army eventually improved my marksmanship enough so I could defend myself, at least at short range, but I never won any awards for it. I have, however, taken aim at a number of personal goals throughout my life, and my ability to hit that type of target has gotten slowly better with time and experience. After missing a great many individual bullseyes and hitting a few, I can't recommend any particular technique; some goals call for a shotgun approach, while others require a precision sniper attack.

But my experience has taught me two solid pieces of wisdom that apply in nearly all situations, especially those involving goal-hunting. First, listen to your mother, or at least to *my* mother: if someone else's advice isn't working, follow your instinct and do it your own way.

Second, if you've used up all your ammunition and still not hit your target, it's time for an entirely different approach. Quit trying from a distance, put the gun away, and act like a cat: sneak up on the target from behind and pounce on it. Whatever works for you. Just pick a goal and get started.

Oh, and one more piece of advice: think twice before discussing it with your sister.

❖   ❖   ❖

RIDING LESSON:

If you're having trouble hitting a long-range target,
try aiming at a series of short-range ones instead. You'll
eventually achieve the same goal, and you'll waste
a lot less ammunition in the process.

Up On the Roof

"ARE YOU OKAY UP THERE?"

I looked down at Betsy on the ground. "Yeah. I'm fine, I'm fine. No problem." I picked up the long-handled lopping shears from the roof and stretched as far as I could toward a branch. Moving only from the waist up, I made a tiny lunge and snapped the jaws closed. Heart pounding, I laid the loppers aside and edged back up. "How much did I cut?"

"A twig and a couple leaves."

This is going to take forever, I thought, working my way down toward the edge of the roof again. *Why in the world am I up here?*

Why else? Because I was cheap. Because I had stretched our budget nearly to the breaking point to buy the house in the first place. Because professional tree trimmers were expensive. Money, or lack of it, was the prime motivating factor for all of our do-it-yourself home-improvement projects. It was also the answer to why I was personally trying to clear overhanging branches off our roof and giving myself heart palpitations in the process.

The real estate listing for our house had stated the problem in two short and emphatic lines: "New second story! High ceilings!" Adding those two things together, you end up with an extremely high roof with a steep pitch. However, I had no reason to add those factors until I was up on top, feeling the grit from the asphalt shingles sliding under my bottom as I edged slowly toward a drop-off twenty-three feet above the lawn.

My experience with the dizzying height of the roof began the summer after we moved in. The trim needed painting, so I analyzed the situation from the ground and announced my plan confidently: instead of constantly repositioning a ladder and climbing up and down dozens of times, I would simply hang over the edge with a brush and finish in a matter of hours. Conceding the project might be a bit risky, I bought a rope, planning to tie it around my waist, run it up over the ridge, and fasten it around a solid object on the ground.

"Oh, that doesn't sound dangerous at all!" said my wife, trying to hide a grin. She had experienced a few of my "great ideas" before. "Why don't you just tie the rope around your neck while you're at it? The end will come a lot quicker that way, and probably be less painful in the long run."

Always a doubter in the crowd, I thought, heading up to the roof for a test run.

Straddling the ridge with a coil of rope, I realized I was high enough to see into the next county. I slowly edged my way toward the peak overlooking the front yard, gripping the ridge tightly with my thighs. Peering down from my precarious position toward the sidewalk a mile or so below, I had the acute sensation I was only one stiff breeze from death. Maybe, just maybe, I could manage to haul a bucket and a brush up there, but hang over the edge and paint? What would I hold on with? My teeth? My scheme might work, but it's hard to scream for help if your mouth is full of shingles. I abandoned my foolish painting plan and prayed I'd never have to climb up on the roof again.

It was a false hope. Shingles don't last as long with tree branches resting on them, and our four large maples kept growing, engulfing one side of the roof in a green cloud of leaves. I could see the roof slowly blackening under the canopy, and dollar signs flashed through my mind. If I couldn't stand to sit up there, how much would a roofer charge to walk around with a load of shingles? I wanted to postpone that expense as long as possible, which meant one thing: trimming the branches.

The first time wasn't too bad; I concentrated on the parts I could reach without stretching too far and hacked the small, leafy twigs off the upper portion of the roof. Unfortunately, this left the main branches intact, and two short years later they once again pushed forth a forest of leaves.

So here I perched again. As I looked down at my wife patiently observing from below, I realized with dismay I was going to be doing this every two years if I didn't move closer to the edge. I simply had to work into a position where I could cut back the big branches.

"Why are you just sitting there?" she asked.

Because I'm paralyzed with fear! I thought. "I'm examining my options," I said. I wanted her to understand the peril of my situation, yet I didn't want to say anything out loud that could be taken as a sign of cowardice.

"I think this is all I can reach," I finally stated in a calm voice. "I'm coming down."

"A few twigs? There's a lot more that needs to be cut, you know."

Not today, I thought. I slowly turned around and began to edge backward down the steep pitch. As I did a toes-first slide toward the drop-off, I was struck with the sudden fear I would miss the ladder and go right over the edge. *Oh no!* I thought as I braced my feet to stop. *We don't have rain gutters to clutch onto!* I could imagine my fingers trying to dig into the asphalt shingles like claws, grasping for anything to stop my fall.

"Honey . . . am I aimed at the ladder?" I tried to sound unconcerned.

"Yes. It's still right where you put it."

"Are you holding it?"

"Yes, dear." She was definitely being tolerant, but sounding amused. "You realize, don't you, that your foot is only about six inches away from it?"

Which means I'm six inches from the edge, too! I thought. I slid down slowly, feeling with my feet for the top rung of the extension ladder. *There are good reasons people get paid for doing this.*

I stopped again. "Are you still holding it?" I panted.

"No, I went inside for a drink of water."

Great. Sarcasm.

I scooted the final few inches over the edge and started down the ladder. I hated feeling so exposed on the roof, but the worst part was that Betsy couldn't appreciate what I was going through. Once I got on the ground I could see her point of view; the roof simply didn't look very high from the lawn, and, sarcasm aside, at least she had been standing by to reassure me.

It's a predicament we see quite often: one person in a difficult position, with spectators watching but not fully appreciating the gravity of the situation because they don't have the same perspective. Physical danger isn't always involved, yet something about roofs seems to bring the difficulty into sharper focus. I thought about this as I put my loppers away, and I recalled a story shared with me by my neighbor, Pete.

Pete was enrolled at a local college and held down a part-time job as well. Recently he had come home from the night shift in the darkness of early morning. Hoping to catch a few hours of sleep before class, he had gotten ready for bed. About to slide between the sheets, he remembered something he had left in the car. In his pajamas and slippers he went back outside to retrieve it. *Sure is cold tonight,* he thought as he returned from his detached garage, stepping cautiously through the darkened yard to his back porch.

He grasped the doorknob. Locked. With the keys inside. And his wife away for the week.

Try the other door, he thought, hopping through the frosty grass of the side yard to his front porch. Locked, too. *This is not good.* Pete began to shiver. *Try the windows.* He felt a definite chill setting in as he checked each opening on the first floor and found everything locked. *This is really not good.*

Pete knew he had not locked his bedroom window, and it appeared to be his only hope of sleeping somewhere besides the garage. Therein lay a problem, however: his bedroom was on the second floor. Toes slowly going numb, he climbed a fence and scrambled to the porch roof to attack the window.

Pete set to work, attempting to pry the old sash window up by pressing his fingertips against the top of the frame. He worked from side to side, trying to overcome years of paint accumulation.

"Pete!" A loud voice echoed between the silent houses, startling him. Pete turned and peered through the darkness at the house across the street. The voice belonged to Burt, heading out to his early shift at the mill.

"Pete!" He yelled again. Burt happened to be a veteran of the neighborhood and a good citizen, always on the look-out for suspicious activity. "Pete! Are you locked out?!" He was leaning forward, trying to peer through the shadows cast by the dim street light.

You think I'm up here for my health? thought Pete, shivering and amazed Burt was yelling such a question. *I'll ignore him.*

"Pete! Are you locked out?!" Burt never allowed himself to be ignored, and he was very conscientious; from the perspective of his driveway, he could see a man in pajamas trying to force his way into his neighbor's window at three o'clock in the morning. It might be Pete, but then again it might not. Something definitely felt wrong, and a good neighbor doesn't let such strange happenings go without positive identification. "Pete! Are you locked out?!"

Pete, wishing desperately to be inconspicuous as he broke into his own home, turned and mouthed the word "Yes!"

Why, the guy's making faces at me! thought Burt. The unidentified person looked a lot like Pete, yet he couldn't be certain. For all he knew, Pete lay sleeping inside, unaware a prowler lurked only inches from his bed. He yelled again, "I say, Pete! Are you locked out?!" Burt could be plenty loud when he wanted to be heard.

Pete, seeing a few lights starting to come on down the street, realized Burt would not leave without an answer. He turned once again from his prying and whispered hoarsely, "Yes! I'm locked out!"

It wasn't loud enough to be heard across the street, and Burt was growing more concerned. "PETE! ARE YOU LOCKED OUT?!"

More lights were coming on in neighbors' houses and Pete could take it no longer. Standing up, he turned and spread his arms wide, white pajamas shining in the glow of the street light. "YES!" he shouted. "YES, BURT! I AM LOCKED OUT!"

Silence for several seconds. *Now what's he going to do?* wondered Pete.

"OKAY!" shouted Burt. He had a positive identification on his neighbor, so he gave a cheerful wave, hopped in his car, and drove away, satisfied it would be another quiet morning on the block.

And there stood Pete, shivering, as curious neighbors peered out their windows at the idiot on the roof in his pajamas.

After my own experience trying to cut overhanging branches, I completely understood Burt's position; sane people don't crawl around on roofs. If you ever see anyone on a roof, you can't assume they *want* to be there, especially if they are not dressed for the occasion. I gave Burt full credit for at least recognizing something might be amiss and insisting on proper identification. How many people would have done the same?

As I pondered my next approach to my overhanging branch problem, I thought about the fact that seeing a man on a roof is similar to encountering a person in the midst of a difficult position in his or her life. From the perspective of an observer, the situation doesn't look too bad. To the person with a problem, however, danger lurks in every direction and each move is open to public scrutiny. Even the possible routes to safety involve danger, similar to one's sliding over the edge of a roof, groping toward an unseen and possibly non-existent ladder.

When we see someone in a difficult situation of any kind, our actions say a lot about what kind of person we are. As Burt did, it's a good idea to check on a person, or at least make sure he intends to be in such a risky position. If you don't ask, he may be hesitant to speak up and request help. And if he needs assistance, go the extra mile to hold the ladder; a steadying hand can make a big difference when someone is taking wobbly steps. Besides, if you don't check on a person, there's always the risk he'll do something really stupid—another insight I have gained from personal experience.

I tackled the branch problem again from a different angle the following weekend. I needed to finish the job, and the solution, I decided, was to cut the offending branches off at the trunk. I soon found myself in a distressingly familiar situation.

This seemed so simple on the ground, I thought as I tried to balance at the top of the ladder at its fullest extension. *Why did I think this would work? Oh well,* I sighed, bracing myself with my knees, *at least I don't have as far to fall.*

My wife, watching once again from the bottom of the ladder, said "Are you okay up there?"

"Yep. Doing great!"

I yanked on the pull start and the chain saw kicked to life, engulfing me in a small cloud of white smoke as the ladder rocked from side to side. "No problem!"

❖   ❖   ❖

RIDING LESSON:

The roof is always higher than it looks from the ground.

TAPS

"READY!"

Rifles clattered as bolts were drawn and cartridges slammed into breeches.

"Aim!"

At Sergeant Hill's command, my soldiers raised the barrels of their weapons, sighting on a distant point in the clear blue sky.

"Fire!"

Seven shots sounded as one, splitting the hot stillness of the August afternoon. I observed the scene from a distance as the first volley of the twenty-one gun salute rolled across the river and echoed off a nearby ridge before fading into silence.

"Ready!"

My squad leader quietly barked the command to begin the second volley, and seven smoking casings popped out of the chambers onto the dry grass. Thirty yards down the hillside, by the open grave, I could see the widow standing with the pastor and a small group of family. She stood clutching a white lace handkerchief against her black dress, occasionally lifting it to wipe her eyes. Her bent form looked small next to the large mahogany casket.

Such a contrast, I thought, looking at her mourning dress against the American flag precisely draped over the dark casket. The stars seemed to be glowing in the mid-day sun, the red and white stripes vibrant.

"Aim!" Rifles pointed skyward again.

Except for the lace handkerchief rising to dab a tear, no movement stirred among the marble and granite headstones of the Fort Riley military cemetery. I glanced at the men of my Infantry platoon, the funeral detail down by the grave and the honor guard preparing to fire again: sharply pressed uniforms, polished shoes, gleaming medals. Perfect. My platoon sergeant had made sure of that before we left the barracks, making it clear no one would ever accuse Second Platoon of bringing dishonor to the dead.

"Fire!" Seven more shots sounded, then echoed back.

No one liked being the duty company, but each unit had to take its turn. The funeral detail may have been the least-favored job of all, yet the task had fallen to my platoon to be on call for two weeks, polished and ready. They had run through the drill dozens of times on the parade ground, repeating the precise actions until they were automatic and perfect. They were ready when the call came down from headquarters, advising that a veteran who had passed away in a nearby town was to be buried in the post cemetery.

Sergeant Hill gave the command to begin the last volley.

No, funeral detail wasn't the favorite duty, but my soldiers understood the significance of their assignment. A veteran is entitled to a burial with a flag-draped casket; it was a right and a privilege belonging to those who had served their country in the military. One day in the distant future that privilege would belong to my soldiers, now standing motionless between the rows of weathered headstones.

The veteran being interred had served his time during World War II, rising to the rank of corporal before his discharge. One day, many long years ago, he had stood at attention, raised his right hand, and repeated the words I had only recently uttered to begin my own service: a solemn oath to support and defend the Constitution of the United States. Not many jobs begin with a swearing-in ceremony, and as a new second lieutenant in my first assignment with "Charlie" Company, Fifth Battalion, Sixteenth Infantry Regiment, I hoped I could live up to the challenge. My regiment was part of the First Infantry Division, a unit with a long and proud history

The veteran had served in the Army for only a few years, yet the memories from his enlistment must have lived with him through the many decades that followed. After only a brief period of service as a young man, he had gone on to spend long years in some other profession—yet here he was, at the time of death, returning to Army soil for his eternal rest. I wondered: *Will my service live with me the same way, remaining forever an experience I can't forget?*

The final volley of the twenty-one gun salute rolled across the cemetery, and the spent casings bounced onto the grass. Behind the honor guard a member of the First Infantry Division Band raised a silver bugle to his lips. For a long moment silence hung heavily in the air. Then the first low, mournful strains of "Taps" rose like a breeze in the hot afternoon, growing in strength with each new note.

There is no song that grips me more deeply than the bugled notes of "Taps." I had first heard its compelling call during my Boy Scout days, sitting near the glowing embers of a dying campfire, listening to the clear, distinct notes soaring quietly over dark and distant pines. A hush always followed, and the solemn effect on the boys of my troop was eerie. I had not known at the time that "Taps" was also played at military funerals, yet somehow I sensed the significance of the piece. Hearing it now brought back memories reaching far back into my youth.

As the song reached its highest note, I could imagine all the soldiers who had gone before me closing their eyes and bowing their heads in respect. For the first time, I heard something in the haunting melody I had never heard before; something unspoken, perhaps a question. As the song trailed off, its last notes hanging in the air, I strained to understand.

Then it was gone. The funeral detail was moving by the grave, lowering the casket into the waiting earth. As the veteran descended to his final resting place, the soldiers stretched the flag tightly above the casket and began folding it. *The flag remains,* I thought. *He is laid to rest, but the flag remains.* The question asked by "Taps" stirred in my mind, still unsaid, yet almost at the level of recognition.

The funeral detail finished folding the flag into a blue, star-studded triangle. As the sergeant handed it to the grieving widow, he slipped three polished brass casings, representing the three volleys of the twenty-one gun salute, into the last fold. With a final glance at the grave, she turned and walked slowly away, clutching the flag and her white handkerchief to her breast.

JUST AS "TAPS" SIGNALS the coming of night on a military post, "Reveille" begins the day a few hours later when it is played with the raising of the American flag. Anticipating its vibrant notes shortly after the dawn of the next day, I stood on the First Brigade parade field in the bright sunshine of a Kansas morning. Third Squad was on color guard duty. I watched them march smartly out the door of the headquarters building, carrying the items for the ceremony: a folded flag and a charge for the cannon. They placed the blank charge in the old howitzer by the flagpole and stood at attention, waiting for the first strains of music to sound across the parade field.

Their actions were confident and precise, once again due to my platoon sergeant's training. I could hear his voice as he ran the squad through their rehearsal, correcting the slightest detail of how they performed their duties, right down to the way they said the name of the song. "It's 'Rev-uh-lee,' men," he had barked in exasperation after hearing it said a dozen different ways. "So quit butcherin' the pro-nunciation—it's disrespectful."

The squad had perfect timing; within a minute, they were clipping the flag's grommets to the lanyard and raising it briskly to the blast of the cannon and the crisply bugled notes. *The flag could almost be the same one as at the funeral yesterday,* I thought. *The veteran fell, was laid to rest, but the flag rises the next morning as if nothing happened. The Army, and everyone in it, goes on as usual.*

Watching the flag snapping in the breeze, I was suddenly struck by the thought that it didn't seem fair. Soldiers died and were buried, yet the flag remained above: aloof, never falling, never soiled by touching the ground that men fought over. The question I had heard whispered in the playing of "Taps" the day before crept back into my mind. I strained to hear more clearly this time, and I suddenly sensed I could put words to it: "Was it worth the price?"

Was it? I wondered. *Did it matter? The hardships of military service, the high price exacted by the oath of office, the dying for one's country? Or not only the dying, but the serving of our country at all?*

Was it worth the price?

Or was that even the question? I couldn't be certain, yet I knew it was a question I must answer. Was my own service worth the price?

The last notes of "Reveille" still seemed to be drifting on the breeze as Third Squad marched back across the parade field with the spent howitzer charge, the smell of burnt powder rising from the blackened canister.

I HAD NOTICED the Manhattan, Kansas, cemetery several times since moving to town. The city of Manhattan is about half an hour from Fort Riley, and I drove by its cemetery on the way to work each morning. It was shaded by large, old trees and surrounded by stone walls with stately wrought iron gates. After seeing the funeral service on post, I suddenly felt compelled to visit this final resting place near my apartment. *Maybe,* I thought, *the answer to my question is there.*

I visited the aging landmark with my wife, Betsy, one weekend. The words inscribed near the gate dedicated the land to the town's fallen Union soldiers, revealing the era in which it had been founded. A paved road led to a beautifully maintained mausoleum at the center of a cemetery filled with many ornate stones and imposing slabs of granite and marble. I felt drawn to more common markers, though. A few steps inside the gate stood a grouping of headstones that spoke volumes to me; not answering my question, but adding to it.

Forming three sides of a square were a dozen or more grave markers, arranged as if the deceased were standing in a military formation. The headstones were plainly inscribed with names and dates of birth and death, and with letters showing they had all served in the same regiment in the Civil War. Most had been born within a few years of each other, but the final dates inscribed on the stones ranged over the last decades of the 19th century, an engraved image of loyalty that lasted beyond life.

I read each of the inscriptions, and a story of young boys growing up together in this small Kansas town began to unfold. In my mind they were barefoot, running through the hot summers of their childhood untouched by the concerns of adults, hardly old enough to shave when the war broke out. A call for volunteers to form a regiment found them kissing their sweethearts good-bye and marching off to the strains of a band and a flutter of flags; marching away from their youth forever, toward a destiny they could not imagine.

Their families read reports of far-off battles in the newspaper and waited expectantly for mail from the front. Mothers treasured the occasional letters, holding onto each word as their only fragile link to their sons and praying the messages, however infrequent, would never stop.

Four years later the soldiers returned, children no longer, aged beyond their years by the horrors of battle. They were much fewer in number; many of their lifelong friends were buried somewhere over the Appalachian Mountains, resting where they had fallen from the sting of a ball or the flash of a cannon. Some survivors carried the pain of wounds with them every day, and none of them could ever forget. They couldn't forget the terrible hardships, the crushing defeats, or the hard-fought victories—and they couldn't forget each other.

One by one over the course of years they died, and the remaining veterans came to stand quietly in the cemetery to pay last respects and say good-bye. With each passing, the living saw their future, knowing one day they, too, would lie in the ground on which they stood. The numbers remained constant, the living gradually being replaced by gray stone markers as a final formation gathered on the other side of life, waiting for its last member to arrive—

waiting for the regiment to stand again, together, whole, as it did in their youth.

There came the day when there was only one veteran, standing with head bowed, then none. And the regiment marched away, to somewhere the world could not follow, as dust settled on the stone reminders of a fading past.

"Was it worth the price?" I asked quietly.

Were you pleased, you who went first, with the reports of those who followed? With the stories of a country rebuilding, of a Kansas town growing, of a nation uniting? You paid the price, each of you, in some way. Was your service and sacrifice worth it?

Betsy wondered at my quiet mood, but didn't ask as we drove away.

"IT JUST SNAPPED, and faster than you could see, it wrapped around 'im. I'll never forget it." My Platoon Sergeant dragged on his cigarette, smoke curling around his head in our small office.

"Was the cable stretching? Could you tell it was about to go?" I asked. The red and white banner of the reconnaissance platoon, my second assignment at Fort Riley, hung behind his desk: cavalry colors originally used by our horse-mounted predecessors, now flown over tracked fighting vehicles.

Sergeant Thompson shook his head in the rising curl of smoke. "No warning. There never is." He would know, since he had recovered dozens of heavily armored troop carriers from the mud during his years in the Army. He paused and looked down at his hands. "I held him for a while, until the medevac chopper got there."

I had heard about the fatal accident that had happened two years before I'd taken over the scout recon platoon, but never a first-hand account from someone who'd been there. As with so many serious situations that happened during training exercises, the procedure appeared routine at first, then confusing, then deadly. It began with a "track" — as the Scout Platoon called their vehicles — caught in a mud hole up to its troop door. Another track was hooked up with tow cables to pull the first one out, the soldiers working by feel and flashlight in the dark of a moonless night. Not enough — the stuck track wouldn't budge. Urgency set in: the mission must go on, other units were counting on them.

A third track was hooked to the first two, and too many people got too close trying to make it work. The diesel engines were powerful, something you could easily forget as you worked around them every day, and the rpm's edged up slowly as they strained against the short cables. In a flash the tragedy had happened: the sound of the snapping cable didn't even register over the noise of the tracks, but a private fell, struck by a one-inch-thick braided-wire whip. Sergeant Thompson would never forget it.

Not even in combat, I thought. *Just training. A cold dark night when everything went wrong, and a kid fell dead in the mud, surrounded by diesel fumes and twisted cable.*

It was the same story I eventually heard in every one of my assignments in the Army; only the details were different. The circumstances were rarely heroic, just deadly. Anyone who had been in for more than one enlistment could tell a story of how someone died in training. Even more were injured, some permanently.

Most veterans never saw the face of combat, never put their continuously honed skills to the ultimate test. Yet they still faced danger, every day, due to the very nature of their jobs. I heard of more tragedies during my next assignment with the Second Ranger Battalion: parachuting fatalities, helicopter crashes, live-fire mistakes. By the time I left the Army I could recount dozens of stories; stories of death or injury in addition to those of the soldiers lost in the wars and battles of my time: Grenada, Panama, the Gulf. In peacetime or in war, the military was a dangerous business.

As I drove away from my last post, Fort Lewis in Washington State, the question still haunted me: Was it worth the price? I felt proud to have served, enjoyed every challenge, developed memories to last a lifetime, but still the question remained unanswered.

Was it worth the price?

Maybe, I thought, *the question doesn't have an answer in the military. Maybe it shouldn't have an answer there, in the world I'm leaving. Soldiers exist to serve, to do what they're told, to follow orders — not necessarily to question. Trust in the chain of command, and save the big picture for when the job is done.*

The answer, I felt, should lie ahead of me in the civilian world I was entering. The civilian world was the entire reason for the military existing; it was the way of life being preserved, the families being kept safe in their homes, the values of freedom being safeguarded. There, in the world populated by many Americans who had never worn a uniform, should be the answer I sought. The whole country had been so supportive of the military effort in the Gulf War, with flags flying and yellow ribbons tied, that surely a current of feeling still flowed strongly through the hearts of Americans everywhere. Patriotism, I hoped, would continue to be on open display.

MY DISAPPOINTMENT dawned slowly. It started, for me, with the flags.

In all my years in the Army, I never saw a ragged one, a stained one, a faded one. The rituals of respect for the banner of our country governed every day on a military post. The work day didn't start until Old Glory was snapping in the breeze, and no matter what you were doing at five PM, you stopped while it was being taken down. At first it had seemed strange to see an entire post, a small town, come to a halt each evening at the sounding of "Retreat" and the lowering of the flag. Cars stopped in long lines as soldiers stepped out to salute while families and civilians stood respectfully by. Strange at first, yet a ritual I grew to love for the tradition of respect it built.

In the civilian world, the first ragged flag I saw was mounted permanently on the peak of a high roof over the front door of a restaurant. Not equipped to be taken down at night, it showed the rips and stains of years of neglect. It was, I realized, a decoration rather than a symbol of America. I began to see such flags in other places: fading in windows, hanging limply in back rooms, frayed on flagpoles. Not that I saw many of them; in the large city where I lived, displaying the flag was not very common, and the rare sight of one waving from a front porch became a welcome but surprising event. People simply didn't think of regularly showing pride in their country.

Some, however, were embarrassed by the flag — the ones who wouldn't stand and cover their hearts at the playing of the national anthem. And not only the flag, but any show of patriotism, especially if it included a demonstration of support for the military. Sometimes I couldn't blame them, because the only military they saw was the one in the papers and on the news, and it was not the one I had known.

All I heard of the world that used to be my entire existence was of the scandals, the crimes, the wasting of money. The military may have been misused at times in the past, yet that was no fault of the individual soldiers, sailors, or airmen. Where were the stories of the Army I had lived in, the one my father, brother, and sister had joined? Where were the dedicated soldiers, the daily effort, the work days that didn't end until the mission had been accomplished? Where were the unselfish men and women who endured hardships to serve honorably? They didn't seem to exist, from many of the reports I read.

Did the country appreciate what it had? Did it care? I wasn't sure, after spending several years in the civilian world. However, I had a sense, a feeling, I wasn't getting the whole story. Deeper down, behind the rushing traffic and the hectic pace, existed the real emotions of Americans, the pride. Not out in the open, but still there, waiting for a chance to come out on display without shame. Yet the pride was hard to see—impossible, at times.

Was it worth the price? Some questions don't have an easy answer.

THE COURTHOUSE IN Ephrata, Washington, occupied a full city block. Like many small town courthouses, it stood as the most imposing building in the county: several stories tall, solid, and stately. Huge trees, planted generations ago, ringed the lawn and shaded the sidewalks leading to the wide entrance.

Business had brought me to this small town in central Washington State, and for a few days one fall I drove by the seat of county government on my way to meetings. During a lunch break one day, I strolled down Main Street, then around to the stone face of the courthouse. The building was beautiful. Off to one side I noticed a small monument and slowly walked over to examine it.

The large marker was covered with names, dozens of names chiseled in slabs of stone. I suddenly felt as if I had been there before, though I knew I hadn't. I had seen this marker, or one like it, in every small town I had ever visited. Rows of names under an inscription: "To Those Who Have Fallen," or other words of the same sentiment. The monuments were always plainly visible on courthouse lawns, or in the center of town squares, or public parks. They existed,

I knew, in larger cities, but were often blackened by exhaust and difficult to notice from the windows of rushing cars. Newer public buildings in those cities, gleaming structures of steel and glass, usually didn't include a prominent spot for such a monument to fallen home town war heroes.

But they had one in Ephrata, unashamedly displayed for everyone to see. I touched the names with my outstretched fingers. *God bless them*, I thought. Some from rich families, some from poor; farmers, laborers, it didn't matter; they all went. They answered a call to duty like the civil war soldiers in Manhattan, Kansas. And this town remembered them, publicly.

The price of freedom, I thought, *is listed on this monument: the sons and daughters of America.*

Why do the young have to pay the price? Before they even taste freedom, they have to pay for it. Is it fair? I studied the names closely, and shook my head. *Of course not. Life is rarely fair.* Yet I had joined the Army at the same age as the young people memorialized on the stone in front of me, and no one had forced me. I couldn't say why I had felt compelled to serve, but it had been one of the proudest achievements in my life, an experience I would trade for nothing else in the world.

How many young people would go today? The breeze rustled leaves that had fallen from the large trees and stirred the American flag fluttering loosely from the tall silver pole. I looked at the people walking by, unhurried, smiling at me as they passed. I sensed the answer, unspoken but sure: Ephrata would send its share. If duty called, the town would answer. And the ones who stayed would remember them, forever. As they remembered these names of long ago.

Here, right here, is the pride of America, I thought. *Chiseled in stone for everyone to see, snapping in the breeze on a brisk autumn day, smiling at a stranger touching a memorial. Not what you see on the news, but the real sentiments of ordinary men and women.* Out here they openly expressed the true feelings I had sensed under the surface of the city.

In the sophisticated city, people sometimes kept their hands in their pockets at the playing of the National Anthem, but in small towns they weren't so self-conscious. They weren't too proud to show their feelings, to say what they felt. Out here, they erected monuments in front of the courthouse, and spoke from the heart — the heart of America.

But was it worth the price?

As I slowly returned to my own small-town roots, I realized I was drawing nearer to an answer at the same time. I didn't have it yet, but I felt closer, and I would know when I found it. The answer would have to come from inside; a response from my own heart.

"I LIKE THE FOUNTAINS."

Eric said the words matter-of-factly as another shower of sparks cascaded upward into the evening sky. "They are definitely the best."

"Yeah. Definitely the best," agreed Robby, seated next to him on the lawn, arms wrapped around his knees, face tilted upward.

From Mom and Dad's farm in southern Idaho, six-and-a-half miles from town, we could see fireworks displays all around the horizon as each small community across the valley celebrated the Fourth of July. Red, blue, green, and white explosions puffed upward every few seconds, but my boys didn't care; they had eyes only for the much smaller display taking place in the driveway in front of the house.

Exactly how I used to feel, I thought, smiling to myself as the fountain sputtered down into a flickering orange flame. *Fireworks are a lot better when they are only twenty feet away.*

My wife and I had brought Robby, seven, and Eric, four, back to the farm I grew up on for a vacation. Dad bought the largest box of fireworks he could find, and a few extras besides, to celebrate Independence Day. He'd bought more than I had ever seen as a child, but grandchildren have a way of bringing out a very generous nature in adults. I felt only too happy to share in my kids' good fortune.

Watermelon and fireworks. There's no other way to properly celebrate the Fourth. I had enjoyed this tradition at least a dozen times growing up, sitting in the same spot on the front lawn.

"Let's light another one!" the boys shouted as the flame disappeared.

As another multi-colored shower of sparks erupted from the end of a sputtering fuse, I watched their young faces. The lights of the fireworks display reflected from their wide-open eyes, dancing blue, green, red. They were filled with the moment, unblinking.

Stars in their eyes, I thought. Young children, my boys, starting out on a life filled with potential. The reflections in their eyes spoke of dreams to dream, goals to pursue, adventures to chase. *So much yet ahead of them. So much those eyes will see. What will they do with their lives?*

And I had the beginning of the answer to my years-old question of whether the sacrifice was worth the price.

What would they do with their lives? Anything they wanted to. Because Americans lived free, my children would have their shot at the dream. Their dream. To strive, to achieve, maybe to fall short, maybe to succeed, yet they would have their chance. No one would decide their fate but themselves, because America was free. They would not grow up with a destiny determined by ancestry, or class, or money. They would not grow up with a lid on their potential, put in place by a government that assigned them to a certain position in a master plan.

Most important, they would grow up free from the fear of so many in the world: the fear their ideas could land them in prison or lead to their death. This fear of holding a thought and following a cause sapped the energy of humans around the world and kept them from achieving their full potential in life. But not in America. Here, they would be free to speak out, to choose a path, to pray to God. Free to jump, free to run, free to fly rather than cower and hide.

For all the restrictions modern Americans feel, the United States is still more free than any country on Earth. So free we have nearly lost the ability to appreciate it; we take many freedoms for granted that other nations simply don't have. This country is still wide open; maybe a bit rough around the edges due to constant change, yet opportunities abound. My kids, or anyone, could start with nothing but dreams and succeed beyond their wildest imagination.

Problems? Sure, plenty of them. But all the problems in America were caused by people, and it's people who are fixing, or at least working on, every one of them. Maybe my kids would be part of the solution. Only they could determine the role they would play, but at least their country, the United States of America, wouldn't hold them back.

Was it worth the price? The answer was in their eyes, not mine: Yes.

Yes, it was worth the price. The years of service, the answer of the call to duty, the sacrifices of the families. Throughout history, mankind has rarely established free societies, and it is no accident it has occurred in America. Our freedom is the result of a solid Constitution and countless millions of soldiers, sailors, and airmen who have raised their right hands and sworn an oath to protect and defend it—men and women who have endured years of service, in peacetime and in war, protecting freedom so the rest of the country doesn't have to worry about it.

As demonstrated by the puffs of fireworks all around, a lot of people in the country agreed with me. It may not be in the news every day, yet it was there: pride.

My children had stars in their eyes. Yes, it was worth the price.

Thank you, God, I thought, as the last sparks of a family fireworks show settled to the driveway. *Thank you for making me an American.*

CLARENCE YINGST IS buried next to his wife, Thelma, in the small cemetery in Jerome, Idaho. My mother's parents, side by side for eternity, had been laid to rest in my home town many years before my own children were born. I had called him "Grampie" as a boy, and he had died when I was still in grade school. To me he had been a grandfather; to his country he had been a veteran. I hadn't known it until I grew much older, but Grampie was another American who had stepped forward and served his time as a young man before spending the rest of his life as a farmer.

I had been to the grave before, yet this time I came for a special reason. Nearly a decade before, I had stood at attention on a hot afternoon in the Fort Riley military cemetery and listened to the mournful strains of "Taps," a question forming slowly in my mind. I had thought about the question for years. I now felt I owed my answer to the veteran my platoon had buried as I began my years of service. My grandfather was a connection to that soldier of the past, and to any others who might be waiting for a report on the direction of the country.

My answer was simple, stated without fanfare, yet with a conviction that had taken a decade to achieve: *Yes. It was worth the price.*

I looked at Grampie's modest, granite headstone. Born November 26, 1891; died September 20, 1973. On the spot where I stood, a veteran had been laid to his final rest. I had been too young to attend the funeral, but I could picture the scene: the dark, wooden casket, my grandmother standing with her children, the cool stillness of an autumn afternoon. The service had been simple, with no honor guard or twenty-one gun salute, but as I stood quietly, my mind drifting, I could almost hear the bugled notes of "Taps" lifting over the surrounding fields of wheat and corn.

As the melody played in my mind, I slowly realized that although I had finally answered my question, there was something much deeper I had been missing. All those years that I had been searching to satisfy only myself, "Taps" in its haunting familiarity had been asking another question from the beginning.

The real question of "Taps," unspoken yet clear if one truly listened, was the same every time its music was played as evening settled, or a casket was lowered. The question which hung in the air as the last note faded was simple: "And what of 'Reveille?'"

"Will the bugler call 'Reveille' in the morning? Answer the question, America, as you go to rest, in your beds or in your graves, your part of the story done for the day or forever: Will the sun rise in the morning on a free country? Will the Republic still stand tomorrow?"

That was the question of "Taps." Not self-serving and of the past, as mine had been, but noble and of the future. And it demanded an answer, an answer that all veterans of the past, those who had served, wanted to hear. I thought of everything I had seen and experienced in my still-young life. I thought of my comrades-in-arms, of their service and sacrifice. I thought of the flags and the fireworks, and an answer came easily.

I looked at his grave, this man I had known for too brief a time, and spoke to him in my mind: *Grandfather, at least one veteran stands before you with an answer. You may report it to all soldiers who have gone before, and all who will follow.*

The answer to the question of "Taps" is everywhere in this country today, if one takes the time to look. I have seen it in the dutiful service of my fellow soldiers and in the neighborhood flags on the Fourth of July. It's on the monuments beside the courthouse steps, and in the light of my children's eyes. The answer is "yes." The country will sleep free tonight, because the Republic still stands.

And tomorrow, with the morning sun . . . tomorrow, because of you and all the rest who served . . . tomorrow, the flag will rise again.

God bless America.

❖   ❖   ❖

RIDING LESSON:

Freedom: A gift from God that must be safeguarded by man.

Fishing the Blacktop River

BRETT TURNED OFF THE highway into the gravel parking lot and rolled to a stop in a row of cars. He stepped out into the bright sunshine of a southern Idaho morning in June. As he zipped up his jacket he glanced at his watch—7:00 AM. It was the first day of his summer job.

My brother looked around for a moment. *Everything is just like I remember it,* he thought. *Hasn't changed a bit since I worked here last year.* He grabbed his lunch box out of the car and walked slowly across the parking lot toward a small metal-sided building. A black-and-white sign posted over the door stated in plain letters: "Jerome County Weed Department." Brett read the words and shook his head. *Hard to believe I'm already back for another summer.*

Brett's job at the department wasn't glamorous. like all the seasonal workers, my brother was hired primarily to spray weeds along the public highways of the county. Hunting down thistles and other noxious plants involved long hours in the hot sun and constant exposure to pesticide fumes, yet he liked the work well enough to return for a second summer. The job paid better than minimum wage, plus offered an important inducement for his dedication: the employees got to cruise around in big pickups all day. You may need to be a teenage boy to understand, but for Brett the trucks were the best fringe benefit.

The department carried out its mission with a fleet of six big Chevy pickups specially adapted to perform weed patrol. The faded green trucks were equipped with four-wheel-drives and modified to carry 150-gallon tanks in the back for weed spray. Each vehicle had two men assigned: a crew commander, who usually did as little as possible, and a driver, who did everything else.

Brett had been a driver the summer before, and through the long, hot hours of work he'd dreamed of moving up to crew commander. The position paid more and came with certain extra benefits. The commander directed the movement of the truck and also got the thrill of shooting at weeds out the passenger window, using a spray gun attached to the tank in the back by a long hose. The biggest benefit, however, wasn't listed on the job description—the opportunity to take naps on weedless stretches of highway.

Brett opened the door of the headquarters building and stepped inside. To his left was the dispatch room, from which he could hear the gruff voice of his boss echoing off the metal siding. Hal Donaldson, the chief of the entire operation, was acknowledged to be the county's leading authority on weed control. He'd been in the business for many years, and there wasn't a plant he couldn't identify, noxious or otherwise. In Hal's mind, weeds were public enemy number one, and the department stood as the only force keeping them from overrunning the county's highways. Hal measured a husky six-foot-two, had close-cropped gray hair, a ruddy complexion, and a cigar clenched permanently between his teeth. He had a good sense of humor, yet his lined face usually wore a serious expression, because in Hal's mind weed-killing was a serious business.

Brett stepped into the dispatch room where Hal was tapping a pencil against a large map of the county mounted on the wall. A young teenage boy stood behind him, shifting nervously from foot to foot.

"Good morning, Mr. Donaldson," said Brett cheerfully as he set his lunch box on a shelf. "I'm back for another summer."

Hal turned, his cigar bobbing up and down as he spoke. "Well, well, well . . . young Mister Weigle is reporting for duty. It's good to have you back." He shook Brett's hand, then pushed back his straw hat. "I got a piece of good news for you, son. You're being promoted. Effective today, I'm making you a crew commander." He jerked his thumb at the teenager. "And I'm giving you our newest employee to be your driver."

Brett's mouth gaped open, speechless. He hadn't dared to hope for a promotion this year, and now a pay raise and a better position were being handed to him his first day on the job. He repeated his new title several times in his mind and puffed up his chest. *Crew commander!* It sounded good.

"Yep," Hal went on. "I'm putting you in charge of Old Number Five." He lowered his voice reverently. "The oldest rig in the department, and the same one I used to drive when I patrolled the roads." He nodded toward Brett. "I trust you, son. I know you'll treat her right."

"Yes, sir!" barked my brother. "No problem."

"Good!" Hal slapped Brett on the back as he handed him a set of keys from a rack on the wall. "Time to work, Weigle. The sun is shining and the weeds are growing." He put his hand on the shoulder of the new employee. "Meet Chuck Randolph. Orient him to the job and get your rig ready to roll."

As they walked to the equipment shed, Brett sized up his one-man crew. Chuck Randolph had reached an awkward age, all legs and arms attached to a body as thin as a rake handle. His blonde hair was cropped short on top and so close on the sides a casual observer might think he was bald under his baseball cap. A bead of sweat rolled down his freckled nose and dripped onto his white T-shirt.

"You nervous, Chuck?" asked my brother.

"Uh, yes, sir." Chuck jammed his hands into his jeans and scuffed the gravel with his boots. "This is my first real job."

Brett nodded, remembering his first day at the department. "You've been driving for a while, right?"

"Yes, sir. I've got my license right here." He patted his back pocket.

"Good. Pay attention as we go over the truck, because you're going to be the man behind the wheel." Brett opened the large sliding door of the equipment shed to reveal the row of pickups inside. "Here's Number Five."

If Brett had been watching closely, he would have noticed the strange look that came over Chuck's face the moment he saw their rig. it was a look of excitement mixed with sheer terror, and both emotions were caused by the same thing: the prospect of driving a big truck with a powerful V-8 engine.

The reason for his uncertainty was simple. Chuck had actually fudged his driving experience a little, both on his employment application and when speaking to my brother. In reality, he had only picked up his license the week before, and his formal training was limited to three hours on the road in a high school driver education class. His informal training was even sketchier, consisting of driving a tractor around the wide-open fields of his family's farm. That was all. Driving a large truck with a stick shift loomed as a frightening prospect to Chuck, yet at the same time he wanted the experience as badly as any other teenage boy. He did his best to control the shaking of his hands as he popped open the hood to begin the inspection.

Brett had Chuck go down a standard checklist of engine items, then told him to get in the cab to test the emergency flashers and turn signals. Chuck pulled open the door, slid into the driver's seat, and was completely overcome by the prospect of being in control of such a powerful piece of machinery. He sat motionless, hands gripping the steering wheel as a surge of hormones washed through his veins. "Chuck has got himself a truck," he whispered out loud, not quite believing his good fortune. The words sounded so cool he repeated them a few times.

"Hey! Wake up and turn on the lights," yelled Brett from the front of the pickup. He watched closely as Chuck fumbled around for the switch. "Are you sure you've been in a truck before?"

"Oh yes, sir. Lots of times," called out Chuck. "I've been all around my farm. Piece of cake." He smiled reassuringly until Brett turned his back. "Of course," he muttered under his breath, "Dad never lets me drive, but you didn't ask that." When they finished the checklist, Brett told Chuck to pull over to the hose to learn how to mix a tank of spray.

Chuck turned the key in the ignition and Old Number Five rumbled to life. Drawing on his tractor-driving experience, he pushed in the clutch and forced the shifter into first gear. He tapped on the accelerator, eased out the clutch, and felt the truck lurch forward. Chuck managed to get the rig stopped by the hose and let the powerful engine idle as Brett demonstrated how to measure the pesticide and water into the tank. As they were finishing up, Hal walked out with a slip of paper.

"Listen up you two. Here's your first assignment. Turn left on Highway 99 outside the parking lot, go down ten miles to Franklin Road, and spray from there all the way to the county line." His voice became even more serious than usual as he pointed at the highway, which ran right outside the department's chain-link fence. "That's the busiest road in the county, so be careful." He patted the truck and said in his gruff voice, "Wouldn't want my old truck to get banged up, you know."

"Okay, Mister Donaldson," Brett nodded. He motioned Chuck into the driver's position and climbed into the passenger seat. *Everything looks completely different from this side,* Brett thought as the truck gave a small lunge and began to creep toward the gate. *It must be the view of a commander.* He settled into the worn vinyl of the seat and draped his right arm out the window like all the veteran employees did. *A soft seat and a ten-mile trip to the first weed. Could be time for a snooze.*

The truck died as Chuck tried to keep it moving toward the gate.

As long as this kid can drive, thought Brett, watching attentively as Chuck started the engine and lurched forward again in first gear. Chuck crept out of the gravel parking lot onto the highway, then gave it some gas for the shift into second gear. He struggled to coordinate the movements of both feet on the pedals as his right hand pulled on the floor-mounted shifter. With only a little grinding the transmission popped into gear and the truck began to pick up speed. *So far, so good,* thought Brett.

Chuck revved the engine, then went for the shift to third. The resulting screech from the gear box was painful to hear, but Chuck persevered, beads of sweat popping out on his forehead. With a final shove, he located the proper slot and the truck suddenly leaped ahead, working its way toward forty miles an hour.

Chuck wiped the perspiration from his brow with the back of a gloved hand, stomped in the clutch and made the final straight shift into fourth gear. They were soon cruising at full speed and he relaxed his grip on the wheel.

Brett had watched the entire sequence closely. *He's driving as well as I did when I was new,* he thought. *Good enough for me to sleep, anyway.* "Do you know where we're going?" he asked.

Chuck nodded. "Straight down to Franklin Road. No problem, sir."

Brett rested his chin on his hand and gazed out the side window at the fence posts whizzing past at regular intervals. *Yes, it is definitely good to be the commander.* His thoughts drifted off to the subjects that normally occupy teenage minds, and within a few minutes the passing scenery began to blur in his eyes.

Chuck smiled, knowing he had smooth sailing for ten miles. Slowly, the speedometer crept up to fifty, then fifty-five, and a sense of power began to build in his adolescent mind. It was nothing more than the delusion of an amateur who has gained temporary control over a complicated situation, yet it was an intoxicating feeling. For the next several minutes as he cruised along the two-lane highway, Chuck imagined himself king of the road.

His confidence was short-lived. As the truck came over the top of a big hill at the seven-mile mark, a scene unfolded that turned his fearless attitude to panic. At the bottom of the hill about a quarter mile away, a big red tractor had stopped on his side of the road. It had been pulled as far to the right side as possible while the farmer worked on the engine, but its large dual tires nevertheless filled more than half the lane. Chuck tightened his grip on the steering wheel as his mind struggled to sort out the situation.

Plenty of room existed to swerve around the obstacle, except for one thing—in the oncoming lane was a large blue truck with a long silver tank on the back, going as fast as Chuck. A sinking feeling grew in the pit of Chuck's stomach as it became obvious both vehicles would arrive at the tractor at exactly the same moment.

To fix the situation, Chuck needed only to slow down, yet in his panic he became strangely hypnotized by the approaching tragedy. His arm muscles tensed, his jaw clenched, and his thoughts started to freeze in his brain. White-knuckled hands gripping the wheel, gas pedal pressed to the floor, he stared straight ahead without breathing. Unnoticed, the speedometer needle crept toward sixty miles per hour as the downhill slope began to increase his speed.

The violent vibration of the accelerating truck slowly awakened Brett from his daydream. It took him a few seconds, gazing through bleary eyes, to realize something was amiss. The fence posts were his first clue, since they were now flashing by so fast they were a steady blur. He sat bolt upright and looked out the windshield.

"Aaaahhhh!" his scream echoed around the cab. "What are you doing?!"

Old Number Five was nearing seventy miles an hour and still accelerating. Brett's foot pressed into the floor, searching unconsciously for a brake pedal as he braced his arms against the dashboard. Adrenaline flooded his body.

"Stop! Stop!! STOP!!!"

Brett's frantic screams were enough to jar Chuck from his paralysis, but there was a lot to do and not much time to do it. Precious seconds were lost as his left foot tried to distinguish the clutch from the brake, and his mind struggled to recall the shifting sequence in reverse order. His thoughts spun in circles as his commander alternated screams with imaginative but unhelpful words. Chuck finally managed to take his right foot off the gas, but it was too late—they had passed the point of no return. The red tractor loomed directly ahead, the tanker truck filled the other half of the road, and only a narrow space existed between the two. Chuck aimed at the gap and both boys held on tight, hoping they would make it through unscathed.

It's common knowledge where I come from that you can't fit three vehicles into two lanes at one time. If you're foolish enough to try such a maneuver, you've got to expect some pretty drastic consequences. The next few seconds were a little hairy as each vehicle dealt with the repercussions of the near collision. In this case, the tractor got the best result, losing only a bit of rubber from one side of a huge, black tire. The Weed Department crew even fared relatively well, considering what could have happened; besides the outside mirrors of Old Number Five, the only loss was ten years off the life of my brother.

The tanker truck, however, lost the most important thing of all: its center of balance. As the driver tried desperately to slow down, the truck began to sway from side to side, coming perilously close to tipping over. The liquid inside the silver tank slammed first one way and then the other, building up more pressure with each crash into the metal sides. In only a few seconds, the force of the liquid became great enough to blow off the top hatch, revealing it to be no ordinary truck.

A tanker such as this one could have been filled with many products that would have caused fewer difficulties in the current situation. Unfortunately, inside this truck were two things: water, which posed no problem, and fish, which posed a big problem. As luck would have it, the tanker was hauling live trout from a hatchery on the Snake River, heading to the mountains to release them in a fishing lake.

It was a truly remarkable sight: with each crest of the internal wave, a dozen or so beautiful ten-inch rainbow trout shot out the hatch in a geyser of water, leaping first to one side, then the other, and landing with a soft thud on the asphalt. By the time the tanker stopped, a school of about two hundred fish were trying to swim their way up Highway 99.

Chuck finally coordinated his feet well enough to stomp on the brake and stop the truck within a hundred yards. He turned on his emergency flashers and raced on trembling legs to join my brother at the scene of the accident. Chaos reigned, with water filling the roadway from side to side, and fish forming a wiggling carpet across the pavement. Brett and Chuck tried their best to help out, doing the only thing they could think of — grabbing the slippery fish by the tails and hurling them in the general direction of the tanker's hatch. It was no use. On the busiest highway in the county, more than fifty cars skidded through the accident scene in the next five minutes, with predictable results. In spite of everyone's efforts, the unfortunate trout were soon headed for the big lake in the sky.

This is bad, thought Brett as he helplessly watched another car skid past. *Really bad. My first assignment as a crew commander, and it's a disaster.* His assessment was right on target. Inexperience, overconfidence, and lack of attention had combined to create a situation that simply couldn't be corrected by those responsible. *Oh well,* he thought hopefully as he looked at the wiggling fish, *at least it can't get any worse.*

My brother was still relatively young or he would have recognized the error of that thought immediately. *Everything* can get worse — sometimes a lot worse. This particular mess was teetering on the brink of disaster, and it needed only a small shove to send it tumbling over the edge.

Everyone except the farmer had played an active part in this unfolding drama so far, and next came his turn to perform. From his ringside seat, he had witnessed the near-accident, and he gazed with dismay upon the flopping fish. Something clearly had to be done, he knew, and notifying the authorities was the obvious first step. He sprung into action.

Grabbing a scrap of paper and a pencil, he ran toward the tanker truck. Dodging speeding cars and squirming fish to cross the highway proved to be difficult, and he was panting by the time he reached the other side. "Who are you working for?" he yelled excitedly at the truck driver.

"Fish and Game Department," came the shouted reply.

"Do they have a radio?"

"Yep," yelled back the truck driver, and called out the frequency.

The farmer scribbled the numbers hastily on the paper. Stepping carefully and keeping a sharp lookout for traffic, he crossed the highway again and dashed toward Brett and his young driver. The farmer took a good look at the two of them to see who might be in charge before addressing my brother. Brett didn't look absolutely in control at that moment, but at least he wasn't crouching on the side of the road with his head in his hands, like Chuck.

The farmer repeated his questions and made a note of the Weed Department's frequency. A good plan seemed to be shaping up, starting with a quick radio call to those who could begin to set the situation straight. A plan, however, is only as good as its execution, and somewhere on the way back to the tractor the farmer got his wires crossed. With shaking fingers, he flipped on his two-way radio and dialed what he thought was the frequency of the Fish and Game Department. But due to excess adrenaline and unclear scribbling, he actually patched in directly to the Weed Department.

A fish flopped on the road by his tractor and another car raced by. He closed his eyes for a moment in an effort to compose himself before pressing the button on the mike. "Come in, come in!" A note of desperation was evident in his voice. "You got a serious situation out here on the high-way!"

Hal heard the crackling radio from the desk in his office and walked over to the dispatch room in time to hear the farmer repeat himself. He didn't recognize the voice. Curious, he sat down and pulled over a pad of paper and a pencil. "What do we got?" he growled into the microphone.

The farmer immediately responded. "Thank God you're there! I'm out here on Highway 99 and one of your vehicles has been involved in a big accident!"

Hal's tough demeanor was shaken. The department had never had an accident in all the years he'd been in charge. He wasn't sure what to do, so he started by checking the dispatch book to confirm his suspicion of which crew was involved. "Brett and the new kid," he muttered under his breath. He pulled out a fresh cigar, clenched it firmly between his teeth, and struck a match. The flame flickered in his trembling hand as he took a few puffs. Trying hard to sound calm and official, he put pencil to paper and stated matter-of-factly, "Give me a rundown." Then he added, "Do we have any casualties?"

A long pause followed, filled with the sounds of rushing traffic. "What's going on out there?" Hal barked.

The farmer, trying unsuccessfully to stay calm, had stopped a moment to take in the scene outside his cab again. He still believed he was talking to the Fish and Game Department and felt he should be as descriptive as possible. His voice cracked from emotion as he shouted into the mike.

"I'm tellin' ya—you never seen such casualties! They came flying outta the truck and landed smack on the high-way!"

Hal bit off his cigar.

The farmer, who could have been a play-by-play sports announcer, rushed ahead, his words spilling out of the radio speaker. "Oh, Lord, it's so terrible I can barely watch!

They're still laying there flopping around and the cars won't stop! They just keep coming and running over 'em and squishing 'em!"

Hal sat speechless, pencil suspended in mid-air.

The farmer, mindful that he had another call to make, finished up by shouting "Hey, I gotta go, but you know what? You definitely need to send someone out here to clean up this mess!" The radio clicked and went silent.

The situation, having officially gone from bad to worse, could only improve from that point forward. The sheriff, alerted by reports of a fish massacre on Highway 99, soon arrived and began to straighten out the mishap. After posting warning markers at either end of the slick spot, he gave Brett and Chuck a police escort back to the Weed Department—with my brother driving.

Meanwhile, back in the dispatch room, Hal sat by the silent radio in shock. He smoked three cigars down to the butt trying to gather the courage to notify two sets of parents that their boys had died in the service of the Weed Department. Just as he was picking up the phone, the police cruiser pulled up. Hal was so happy to see his employees alive that he ran right out to the parking lot and hugged them. In fact, he was so relieved he hugged the sheriff, too.

The incident on Highway 99 obviously illustrates the importance of clear communication. However, I think there's a better lesson. No matter where our journey is taking us—down the road of life or just down the highway—we have to pay attention, especially if we're not driving. The less control we have over the ride, the more important it is to keep our eyes on the road.

❖   ❖   ❖

RIDING LESSON:

No matter how bad the situation, we can always make it worse if we try hard enough.

It's Time to Grow Up

"LEAVE THE DOG ALONE!"

My voice rolled across the yard and echoed off the neighbor's house, rebounding several times before fading into the distance. The words had staying power because of their source: I had yelled them from the top of a forty-foot ladder leaning against the highest gable of our two-story house.

"Leave the dog alone!"

I waved the paint brush for emphasis, spraying drops of forest green on the lawn below, along with beads of sweat. We had picked the hottest week of the summer to decide we didn't like our house's blue trim, and I was spending my vacation banging a borrowed extension ladder around the house in circles: the scraping circle, the priming circle, and finally the painting circle. It was all I could do to force myself up and down the ridiculously tall ladder, continuously risking my sunburned neck by leaning as far as I could to either side to slap on the paint. The job had turned out to be much larger than Betsy and I had imagined, and we were pushing ourselves hard to finish. "If only we could have an uninterrupted hour or two ...." we kept saying to each other.

"Leave the dog alone!"

But of course we couldn't. Down below, life in our household went on as usual. For starters, our eighteen-month-old son, Eric, had decided that very week to give up his schedule of two long naps a day. Our older son, Robby, was keeping himself occupied by chasing our six-month-old dog in circles with a water hose. The dog, for her part, seemed to be enjoying the game, but the constant barking was starting to get on my nerves.

"LEAVE THE DOG ALONE!"

Kids! They always have to make everything so difficult! There were too many responsibilities, too many projects, too many commitments, and not enough time, energy, or money to do them all. A series of "why's" ran through my mind: *Why did we buy a puppy three months after buying our first house? Why did we decide every project on the list had to be done this summer? Why did we buy paint when we don't even have a week's food in the cupboard?*

And the biggest question at the moment: *Why do our kids always seem to act up when we have something important to take care of?*

"I'm not ready for this," I muttered, climbing down the ladder once again. I seemed to have the full-blown responsibilities of an adult without the knowledge, patience, or money adults were supposed to have so they could deal with such burdens. I had bitten off a lot more than I could chew, and I felt like whining.

The dog trotted over as I sat down on the grass to rest. "These kids are going to drive me crazy," I said out loud, holding the pup's head in my hands. "I'm not ready for this." She looked at me intently for a moment, then licked my nose.

I shook my head, pulled myself up to my feet, and grabbed the ladder to move it again. *Oh, well. Once you start a job you've got to finish.*

I HAD THE SAME doubts the next summer, scarcely more confident in spite of another year's experience. Vacation time had come again, and after twelve long hours of confinement in the car we had arrived at Mom and Dad's house for a five-day break. The dry air and wide horizons of southern Idaho seemed to clear my head for thinking, especially in the early morning. Standing on the back step with a cup of coffee, I looked down at the patio and saw three handprints in the concrete. They had been made by my brother, sister, and me many years before, and our names and ages were scratched under them: Brett—11, Scott—8, Anne—7.

Where did the time go? I knelt down and placed my hand over my old print, completely covering it. *It feels so solid.* I stood and drank my coffee, remembering the day I had pressed my small hand into the concrete. *I wish my life felt as solid now.*

The same thoughts came back to me that I'd had the summer before when I'd painted the trim. I simply didn't feel I was ready for the responsibilities of being a parent. When I was a child my mother and father had seemed so much older and more experienced than I currently felt. *Let's see,* I thought slowly, looking at the numbers scratched into the patio, *when I was eight, Mom and Dad would have been . . . just about my age now.*

Impossible! Mom and Dad had always appeared so confident, so certain. I may not have agreed with them all the time, but I never doubted they were in full control of their own lives as well as mine. *They must not have felt completely ready to raise children, either,* I realized slowly. *I wonder if I'm fooling my kids into thinking I have my life figured out?*

It didn't matter; ready or not, I had a job to do with my children and a lot to accomplish before they grew up. *But why do they make it so difficult sometimes? Almost as if they're fighting what's best for them.*

Betsy opened the back door and poked her head out. "What's going on?"

"I'm looking at this print I made as a kid. Seems like it wasn't very long ago."

My wife stood beside me and looked down at the concrete. "Age eight. Your mom told me a story last night that happened a couple of years before that."

"Which story?" There existed a definite downside to introducing your spouse to your parents. "Was I bad in this one?"

"I'm beginning to wonder if you were ever good." She smiled. "I asked your mom where Robby gets his stubborn attitude, and she told me about the stomachache episode. Do you remember it?"

I remembered. Mom once took me to the doctor in search of an answer to my constant complaints of an aching stomach. After listening to a description of the problem, the elderly doctor rubbed his chin and thoughtfully examined me standing before him, a defiant frown on my face.

I had been quite difficult as a child. The mildest word you could use to describe my young disposition was "cranky," and my mood often turned much worse. My mother was a registered nurse and a woman with a lot of common sense, yet I managed to confound even her at times. I could be such a stubborn and difficult little person in so many ways, she sometimes had difficulty determining the source of my problems.

"Upset stomach, eh?" said the doctor slowly. "What does the boy like to eat?"

"Well," admitted Mom, slowly realizing the direction he was heading, "He has refused to eat anything but baloney and horseradish sandwiches lately."

"I see." His eyes traveled up and down my small form again. "Tell me, Mrs. Weigle, if you don't mind – does he always wear his belt like that?" He pointed at my leather belt, tooled with Indian designs. Although I was a skinny kid, it was cinched up so tight my belly hung over.

"He, uh . . . ." Mom stammered, wishing she could escape the coming judgment. "He insists on dressing himself, and, he . . . he's afraid of his pants falling down."

"Well, that particular pair of pants isn't going anywhere, I'd say," nodded the doctor thoughtfully. He removed his glasses and pursed his lips before turning his shaggy white eyebrows toward my long-suffering mother.

"Mrs. Weigle," the doctor asked slowly, figuring he ought to get directly to the root of the patient's problem, "Are you a first-time mother?"

No, Mom had explained to Betsy when she told the story, she wasn't – but it was the first time she had been the mother of Scott. Very little in the raising of my older brother had prepared her to deal with my stubborn attitude and cranky disposition.

Betsy laughed. "Your mom also told me about the time she warned you not to play bulldozer by running your forehead on the carpet all over the house. You ignored her and did it anyway, for a whole day. She said the scab took two weeks to heal." Betsy looked at my scalp. "No wonder your hair is so thin up there."

Great, I thought. *I have no one to blame but myself for the difficult side of my children.* I could hear the kids inside the house, getting ready to come out and help their grandpa with the morning chores. I drained the last of my coffee. *Well, one thing I know for certain: I'm not likely to get much sympathy from Mom and Dad!*

THE BROCHURE MADE THE sport sound like the perfect activity for our son; a way to learn about baseball and an introduction to the concept of teamwork at the same time. It was the spring after our vacation to southern Idaho, and T-ball season had begun. I had no background in baseball, not being inclined toward the sport when I was young, yet the rules were simple enough to understand. The kids hit the ball off a tee and were allowed to take only one base at a time. Nobody kept score; the kids simply played to have fun.

The brochure stated the guiding philosophy in plain words: "If you're not having fun, make sure you tell your coach!" We read that part to Robby, and he became enthusiastic to begin. We arrived at the first practice with high expectations and no idea of what lay in store for us.

The first T-ball practice will always live in our memory as the most embarrassing hour my wife and I have experienced together. We suffered, as only parents can suffer, through every long minute. As soon as the coach finished his initial pep talk, he asked if there were any questions. Never shy, my son yelled out the first one at the top of his voice: "Where's the bathroom?"

Oh boy, I thought, as I led him to the trees at the side of the field, *this isn't starting out very well.* The real fun was yet to begin.

Out in the field, Robby tried to play every position at once. He fought his teammates for the ball, no matter where it rolled; several times he ran to home plate from left field to claim it. And he didn't simply pick up the ball; he tackled it, rolling on the ground as if it had to be subdued.

His throwing technique was equally unusual: he would wind up dramatically in the general direction of his target and let the ball fly—directly into the ground at his feet. If the batter took too long to get on base, he pouted. If the ball rolled between his legs, he sobbed.

Within minutes, his shirt was untucked, his pants were covered with dirt, and his face was streaked with sweat and tears. We could almost hear volumes of unspoken judgment from the other parents. "What is your problem?!" we hissed at him from the baseline, trying not to attract any more attention to ourselves.

Our words had no impact. Robby was in his own world. "Coach! Coach! I'm not having any fun!" he bawled, repeating the words from the program brochure. Betsy and I wanted to die on the spot. What kind of parents did these people think we were?

With agonizing slowness, the practice finally came to an end, but the image of my son's spectacle didn't leave my mind for hours. After the kids were in bed, I was brushing my teeth and mulling over the day's events. *Robby looked exactly like he was drowning,* I thought, remembering his flailing arms in the outfield.

I stopped brushing and considered that image. *Well, if Robby was really drowning I wouldn't hesitate a second to jump into icy water to save him. I wouldn't worry about what the spectators thought, and I wouldn't feel embarrassed by his thrashing. I would jump in and go.* I looked at my reflection in the mirror and shook my head. *I guess he's in need of rescuing now, just as much as if he were struggling to keep his head above water. And there are only two people who can save him. If his parents don't, nobody else will.*

Having a child automatically sets the priorities in your life, whether you are ready or not. We had committed our son to playing T-ball, and it was our responsibility to help him follow through. Children learn from everything, and Robby was going to learn something from this experience; he could learn a lifetime hatred of baseball, or we could teach him a lesson in sharing, patience, and teamwork. As Mom and Dad had stuck by me, it was my turn to do the same for my own child.

Improving his ability required a mix of discipline and encouragement: we made every practice; we corrected him when he fought over the ball; we cheered him when he came up to bat; we said "stay on your feet" a thousand times as he rolled on the grass. Betsy coaxed him into throwing the ball farther than three feet, and she played catch with him daily.

In spite of our diligence, his technique improved only marginally by the end of the season. There are no quick fixes in child-rearing, just lots of small steps, and we took but a few that year. Robby wanted to play again the next year, so we kept practicing after the season ended, trying to reinforce everything the coach had taught him by playing ball a few times each month.

One weekend in mid-summer I took a break from mowing the lawn to spend a few minutes in batting practice with Robby. He acted difficult from the start, insisting on holding the bat improperly in spite of my constant corrections. My mood rapidly turned sour, and I was trying to maintain a cool head when I heard a voice behind me.

"Daddy, my wet wag is dwy." I turned to see Eric holding out a crumpled blue washcloth.

Aack! I thought. *Not now! I can only handle one problem child at a time!*

Like Robby, Eric was growing up fast and developing his own unique personality. One time when he had come down sick with a cold, we had given him a damp washcloth to wipe his runny nose. His cold had lasted a long time, and when it was over he had adopted his own form of security blanket: wet rags. Of course, he was too young to dampen them by himself, so he constantly asked for assistance.

"Eric!" I turned to him, my voice reflecting the hard edge of my exasperation. "Why are you so obsessed with those stupid rags?!" I looked at him and paused. He appeared so little, standing there with his crumpled rag, yet he had grown an amazing amount in the last year. His childhood was already slipping by, and I had the sudden realization that he was the last one. When Eric grew up, there would be no more kids around.

I didn't want to look back and regret the way I dealt with my children. I wanted to enjoy them, because their time with us was short. *What are they going to remember about their childhood?* I wondered. *Their dad always being in a foul mood? Is that what I want?*

No. I could handle a simple wet rag. I could handle a problem grip on a bat. I could even handle both at the same time. It simply took the correct measure of discipline and a lot of patience. *I deal with ten problems at once at the office, every day, and I never lose my cool. They are kids; I am the adult; I can handle anything they throw at me.* I forced myself to relax. *And I can do it with patience.*

I took a deep breath and started again.

THE BIGGEST SURPRISES in raising children often come on those occasions when we realize our efforts have made a difference, if only a small one. The reason for the surprise is that the changes can be so gradual it is hard to tell they are actually happening. And so another year passed, the seasons turning once again to spring, before we saw the results of a year's worth of patience.

Once again on the same practice field, Betsy and I stood on the baseline as Robby trotted out to play. The difference was amazing: he could throw, he could bat, and he could hold his position on the field when the ball didn't come to him. He still needed work on catching, yet his progress was remarkable. Betsy and I thought his development must be obvious to everyone watching, and we mentioned to one of the other parents how embarrassed we'd been the year before by his awkwardness.

"I don't remember that," she said, turning to yell a correction to her own child. "Kelly, don't fight over the ball. And stay in your position." I laughed and shook my head as I realized we had been so concerned with Robby's behavior we had assumed everyone was judging us. In truth, most of the parents didn't notice a thing; they were too busy being embarrassed by their own kids.

As Robby stepped up to the plate, I looked at Eric swinging a small bat behind us, knocking the heads off dandelions. *Lord, we're trying. But in the meantime, please help these kids survive their parents.*

Most of us have a lot stronger foundation in life than we imagine; we've just never put it to the test. We don't have to be completely grown up to start teaching our own kids the right way to live and behave. In reality, raising children may be one of the last steps in growing up; our kids look up to us as adults, and even if we don't feel we know what we're doing, we have no choice but to start acting like adults. We have to take a deep breath and jump in, especially if our children look as if they are drowning. It's a lot easier to save them when the water is shallow, because the longer we wait, the deeper and more difficult the situation becomes.

One small step at a time, everyone in our family had walked a bit farther along the road of growing up. At the end of the season, the coach announced that Robby was the most improved player on the team. Pride beamed from his smiling face all the way home from the last game.

This child-rearing thing is a full-time job, I thought as I opened the trunk to take out the lawn chairs and put them away. As I bent over to grab the first one, I heard a loud yelp. Whirling around, I saw the dog racing around the yard, Robby in hot pursuit with a hose. Eric was standing by the house, cranking the faucet on full blast.

"LEAVE THE DOG ALONE!"

❖   ❖   ❖

RIDING LESSON:

It's OK to grow up one step ahead of your children.

THE RAFT

I RESTED MY PADDLE against the inflated side of the raft and considered my words carefully. "This is exactly what happens every time I do this in the Army, too."

Silence. My wife and I had been married only a few months, so I was still learning what to say when we got into a disagreement. After the words left my mouth, I realized I had probably guessed wrong; comparing our relationship to the military brought up the wrong mental image.

I tried again. "In fact, this has happened every time I have ever been in a raft with anybody."

More silence. I looked over my shoulder, only to be pierced by her frosty gaze. *Well, what am I supposed to say?* I thought harder. "Listen, why don't you take a break and I'll do the paddling for a while? Relax a little."

I dipped my paddle into the clear blue water of the lake and began pulling toward the lily pads floating in the distance, alternating sides with each stroke. *Inflatable rafts are just difficult,* I thought. *There's no getting around that. They're not streamlined, so they don't go in any particular direction.* Small yellow rafts like the one we were kneeling in could just as easily be paddled sideways, and it was up to the occupants to determine what direction they would go.

And there lay the problem. Having been in rafts before in the Army, I had assumed my experience put me in charge. I had informed Betsy as we shoved off from the shore of the lake that I would take the lead position on our brief excursion. Kneeling in the front end, I stated with authority, "All you have to do is paddle when I do, but stroke on the opposite side."

The arrangement had worked for about ten strokes. Then, feeling the back end swinging off center, I turned to instruct my crew. "Maybe I didn't make this clear before we left. We are trying to go over there." I pointed with my paddle.

"I know exactly where we are going. And I am keeping us aimed in the right direction to get there." Betsy was tight-lipped.

"Well, actually, you seem to keep steering us a little off course." I smiled, hoping to soften my instructional tone. "So, let's pay a bit more attention to my lead, okay?"

In short order, we had arrived at our current position: spinning in choppy circles. It was a common situation in rafts. The one at the back always thought the one at the front was going in the wrong direction, and the one at the front always thought the one at the back was ruining the smooth progress toward the goal.

I turned back to my efforts after suggesting Betsy take a break. Five more strokes, and it became clear from her continued paddling she wasn't in the mood to be a simple passenger. I sighed; the lily pads weren't getting any closer.

"Why don't we head back? There seems to be a bad current out here today." I was starting to wonder if we would even be able to return safely to the shore with two captains at the helm of our small craft. Since I received only further silence, I started to turn the raft around. My intentions were partly motivated by self-interest; having recently sprained my ankle severely enough to require a cast, I didn't know how well I would be able to swim with ten pounds of plaster encasing one leg.

The tension of the raft disappeared as soon as we were back on shore. As we ate lunch at a picnic table overlooking the lake, we were lost in our own thoughts, watching the squirrels chattering at each other in the tall pine trees. *Everything is fine,* I thought, *when two people are in familiar surroundings. It's when you get into uncharted waters that the trouble starts, especially if the boat has no built-in direction and the crew has to agree on where to go.*

Uncharted waters. I smiled. *Those two words sound like a pretty good description of marriage.*

"DEAR BETSY."

I paused with my pen on the paper, not sure how to express my feelings. I was undergoing Ranger training with the Army, and being camped out under a poncho in the desert didn't make for inspired letter-writing. I had met Betsy in college the day before summer break began, and I was hoping I could convince her to see me again when I returned to classes in the fall.

Humor, I thought. *A little humor never hurts in a love letter.* I continued writing. "You can take this into the shower to read since it is written on waterproof paper."

I read it back to myself. *That sounds pretty stupid.* I considered starting over, yet I couldn't think of anything better to say. *She probably won't even want to talk to me again anyway, so what's it matter?* "I've been thinking a lot about you . . . ." I finished writing, ripped the letter out of my pocket notebook, and stuffed the paper into a dirty envelope. Selecting a stamp from my meager supply, I licked the back and pressed it on, but it wouldn't stay, having lost its stickiness from being exposed to the weather for too long. *I hope that's not a bad omen,* I thought. *Now what am I supposed to do?*

I dug around in my backpack and found a roll of black electrical tape, kept on hand for minor equipment repairs. Forming a loop with the sticky side out, I used it to attached the stamp. I crawled out of my shelter and carried the finished product over to the sergeant who was collecting mail.

He looked over the stained envelope and lumpy stamp. "Who are you sending this to?"

"Uh," I stammered, "someone back home."

"'Betsy' it says." He looked at me. "Who's that? Your girl?"

"Well, sergeant, she's not exactly a *girl.*" I couldn't stop stammering. "She's . . . uh . . . a woman, I mean a lady — or whatever. Just someone I met." *And what do you care anyway, Sergeant Snoop?*

He shoved it into the mail bag. "Well, you'll be lucky if she ever looks at you again after seeing that mess."

He's probably right, I sighed, returning to my poncho-covered hole under a bush. *He's probably right.*

Return mail never caught up to me during training, so I arrived back at school in the Northwest with no idea what to expect. I didn't need to worry; my "girl," as the sergeant had called her, was waiting, holding a dirty envelope and looking for me.

We were nearly inseparable from the start, and right away I noticed Betsy caused a power struggle to break out between my head and my heart. I was a logical sort of person, and up to then my brain had been clearly in charge of my life. My mind was always thinking about the next move, constantly planning and predicting exactly where my path would lead. But love turned everything upside down and created a state of confusion that was difficult for a logical brain to deal with.

Ever since my freshman year in college, I had planned to begin my career as an Army officer after graduation without making any commitments. However, even a logical brain can read the writing on the wall, and about a year and a half after meeting her, I began to wonder if I should factor Betsy into my plans. I sat down one night and started a detailed list of the pros and cons of making a long-term commitment, confident such a careful analysis would lead to the right decision. Reviewing the list, I had to admit I had a relationship worth keeping, yet I didn't want to rush into anything.

We'll just put this little romance on simmer, I thought. *After I get established in the Army, we can discuss our relationship together.* Satisfied I had made a solid decision, I put the list away and breathed a sigh of relief, happy I wouldn't have to make any substantial changes to my plan. *I won't mention a thing about commitment for at least a couple of years.*

The next week I proposed to her.

I'm still not sure exactly how it happened. We were walking home from a late movie at the time, so the cool night air might have been the cause, or the glow of the moon, or maybe it was a simple case of fatigue. Whatever the reason, my emotional heart sensed a moment of weakness and overpowered my logical brain. I couldn't stop myself, and I asked Betsy to marry me on the spot. I didn't have a natural flair for either romance or timing, since I proposed to her in the parking lot of a Kentucky Fried Chicken. She didn't seem to mind, though. She *did* mind when she found the pro and con list, so I scraped together enough money to buy a modest ring and that distracted her. We began to make our plans together.

"Do I really have to do this?"

Betsy dialed and handed the phone to me. "Yes. This is the way it is supposed to be done, and we want to start off right."

I sighed and listened to the ringing on the other end of the line, my stomach tightening into an apprehensive knot. Someone picked up the phone.

"Hello?" The voice of Betsy's father sounded forbidding to my nervous ears.

"Uh, hello," I began, my voice nearly cracking from the strain. "This is Scott. So, how are you doing?"

"Fine." I couldn't read his tone.

"Well, I was just calling to talk about something. Something, you know, important." *Charge ahead, Scott. There's no turning back.* "Your daughter — that would be Betsy — and I have decided we're going to get, um, married. And so, I'm calling to ask you for permission to do that."

Silence. I held my breath as several seconds ticked by before he spoke again. "Aren't you supposed to ask *me* before you ask her?"

Oh no! I thought. *He's got me on a technicality!* As I struggled to find words, another voice came on the line. "Who's on the phone?" It was Betsy's mother.

"Scott says he's going to marry Betsy."

"He's what?!"

My reserves of courage, low to begin with, evaporated in a flash of panic. With my mind screaming *elope! elope!* I handed the phone to Betsy and retreated. To my relief, after the initial shock wore off, her parents gave their blessing and we put our marriage plans in high gear.

The day of the wedding is still a blur to me. I recall only a few details, images fixed like snapshots in my mind: pacing anxiously in a small room at the back of the church as the guests were being seated; trading nervous jokes with my best man, a friend who felt as uncertain about his part as I felt about mine; my father sliding around in slick plastic shoes that matched his rented gray tux.

But one image stands out from the rest: my first sight of Betsy, framed by the doorway at the end of the aisle, smiling at me as she held onto her father's arm. Pearls glittered from her veil and her long train flowed behind her as she began to walk slowly toward the altar. She was beautiful, and I could hardly believe she was about to be mine.

We were on a strict budget, and could only afford a short honeymoon at a nearby lake resort. Two days later we packed our meager belongings into the trunk of our car and set off for my officer training course in Georgia. It was the first time Betsy had ever left home without her family, and a tear rolled down her cheek when we drove away from everything she had ever known.

The world seemed very big and we felt very small. As we set off toward an uncertain future, all we had was each other.

A few days later, we heard the first trace of a drawl from our waitress when we ate lunch in Wichita. The landscape slowly changed as we continued our journey through Oklahoma and Arkansas, the dry fields of wheat slowly giving way to lush foliage and thick pine forests. As we crossed the Mississippi River into the Deep South, we began to feel things were a little different from our familiar home in the mountains of the Northwest.

"Goin' swimmin' tonight?" The old man seemed surprised. "Have y'all looked at the pool lately?"

We weren't used to the heat and humidity, and it had taken a large toll on us both. The pool in our apartment complex had looked very inviting after dinner one night, and in the darkness of a Georgia evening, we slipped into our swim suits and strolled over for a dip. We met the care-taker on the way.

"Sure," I replied. "The pool is deserted. Looks like a perfect time to go."

He smiled when he heard my voice. "Ya'll aren't from here, are ya?" He nodded toward the deserted pool. "Well, you two have fun. But be careful in there."

"Be careful?" I said as we took off our shoes. "What's he talking about?"

"I don't know, but I can't wait to get in." Betsy dipped her toe into the deep end. "Oh, it's nice and cool!" She backed up and dove in with a splash. "Come on! It feels great!"

We treaded water together in the dim glow of the pool-house light. "This feels so good," I said. "I don't understand why no one else is in here!"

A low buzzing sounded from the other end. "What's that?" Betsy asked.

"I don't know." It sounded again. "But I think it's getting closer." Neither one of us was wearing our glasses, and our poor eyesight wasn't helping.

"I'll check it out." Betsy swam slowly toward the buzzing noise, trying to peer forward in the darkness. It stopped as she drew nearer. "I don't see anything." She spun in a slow circle. Suddenly something smacked her in the back of the neck. She whipped around and looked directly into a flurry of buzzing wings floating in front of her face.

One scream and two seconds later, we were standing outside the pool. With our eyes adjusted to the dim light and our glasses back on, we could see dozens of floating creatures buzzing in small circles. Any Georgia native could have identified them as cicadas, large flying insects that had been dying and falling into the water for the last week. And like the caretaker, the natives could also have identified *us* without any problem: naive Yankees who didn't know any better than to take a bath with the huge bugs.

The swimming pool was the first indication that we had no idea what we had gotten ourselves into. And the adventure was just beginning.

"Doesn't this look perfect for Christmas dinner?" Betsy held out the recipe book for me to look at.

"What is it?"

"Glazed duck with orange stuffing," she said. "I think it's French. It's filled with chopped oranges, then roasted and covered with an orange glaze. Doesn't that sound perfect for a fancy holiday dinner?"

"Well, I don't think I've ever had duck before. It looks pretty good."

"I've never had it with orange sauce," she said, "but ducks are on sale at the commissary." She sighed. "At least the meal will be special."

Holidays had been the hardest part of being away from home, and it was difficult to stay cheerful as our first Christmas approached. No matter how hard we tried, our best efforts produced only a poor shadow of the familiar traditions of our families. Our budget had allowed only one decoration, a scrawny pine tree that sat on a table to compensate for its lack of height. As we sat planning our feast the tree was already losing its grip on life, its needles littering the few small presents tucked under its drooping branches. However, we now had something to make up for all the deprivations: the duck.

Neither one of us had ever prepared duck before, yet the recipe seemed easy to follow. Betsy worked most of the afternoon, peeling and cutting oranges, and when the bird came to the table, carefully arranged on a large platter, it truly looked like a gourmet dish. She set it down proudly in the center of our modest feast. My mouth began to water, and I carved off a large piece and took a bite. Betsy waited anxiously for my reaction.

"What do you think?"

This, I thought, *is a test. We are two thousand miles away from home, all by ourselves. This is the high point of the day, and my wife spent the entire afternoon preparing our first Christmas dinner.* I managed a smile. *And I have a huge mouthful of orange-flavored duck fat.*

"You don't like it."

Chew! Make yourself chew! I couldn't do it.

"You don't like it!"

Careful, Scott, careful. I smiled harder. *How do I tell her this is the greasiest thing I have ever put in my mouth without hurting her feelings?* "Boy, this is interesting." I said, trying not to gag. "I guess now we know why those ducks can float around in freezing water all day without getting cold."

"What do you mean?" She speared a piece with her fork, popped it into her mouth and chewed once. That was it. The cheerful facade was shattered and a large tear welled up in her eye. Our Christmas celebrations have gotten better every year since, but we have never attempted to cook a duck, orange or otherwise, again.

Our first year, most of it spent in Georgia, was filled with moments of shared adventures and new experiences: fireflies blinking between the branches of moss-covered trees; buckets of sand dollars on a deserted ocean beach; skillet-blackened catfish and iced tea that always came sweet unless you told them otherwise. Ordinary stuff to the locals, but we felt as if we were discovering a whole new world.

Getting married first, before starting out, had been the most important decision we could have made. We had only ourselves to rely on, and turning to each other in all situations became a habit. At the end of several long months of Army training, we packed up our small but growing household and hit the road again. We were no longer newlyweds when we arrived in Kansas for our next assignment.

The wide-open skies and endless horizons seemed to be a perfect match for the confidence we felt in the future. Our relationship became even stronger over the next two years, and we were certain we could handle any challenge the Army, the world, or anybody else could throw at us. We were still too young to know the most difficult trials in life usually don't come from the outside, but are a consequence of personal actions. Without realizing what we were doing, we came up with the true test of a relationship all by ourselves.

"I'll stay up. You go back to bed."

Oh, how I would love that, I thought. I was getting smarter with experience, however, and my mind was generally sharp enough to avoid obvious traps, even at two o'clock in the morning. "No, you go to bed. You need your sleep, too."

Betsy shook her head wearily. "No, as long as he's up, I'm up. But you have to go to work tomorrow."

Thank God, I thought. *Maybe I can sleep at my desk.* I sighed. "Let's see. We've changed him, fed him, burped him, and rocked him. What's next?"

Our first son had been born in an Army hospital on a cold winter day at Fort Riley, Kansas. The birth had come earlier than expected, and I had been out on a three-day training exercise with my Infantry unit. The announcement of my wife going into labor was transmitted over the radio for everyone in the battalion to hear, and I rushed back to the base as fast as the Jeep would carry me.

A few days later we brought home Robert. Betsy felt exhausted, and we both thought the hardest part was behind us. *All we need,* I thought, *is a little rest and we'll be back on track.* He started crying that night, and sometimes, in the early morning hours, it seemed as if he had never stopped.

"We haven't bounced on the bed with him yet."

This is crazy, I thought as I hopped up and down. *But it worked once and maybe a miracle will happen again.* We could have taken turns caring for him at night, but each of us felt guilty when the other was up, so we always stuck it out together. Every once in a while, something would work, and we would collapse back into bed, overjoyed that we had finally found the key to calming the baby. Of course, the same method never worked again, and we simply added it to the long list of techniques we tried each sleepless night. We repeated the same pattern for months.

"That's not working," said Betsy in a bleary voice. "I'll walk him outside for a few minutes."

Getting only four hours of sleep wouldn't be so bad, I thought, *if I could just get them all at once.* As I watched Betsy walking back and forth on the sidewalk with Robby bundled in a blanket, I recalled a conversation with my platoon sergeant the day before. He had laughed when I became excited that my unit was scheduled to go back out to the field for a week of training. He'd raised his own small children, however, and he understood my position. I didn't care that I'd be lying in the dirt under the stars every night; sleep under any conditions would be better than what I was getting.

Betsy came back inside and tiptoed quietly up the stairs. "Shhh . . . he just went to sleep," she whispered hoarsely as she laid Robby in the crib. "Let's go to bed."

The sleepless nights seemed to go on without end. Every new stage in Robby's development upset his sleep schedule, and we did whatever it took to reclaim our lost hours of slumber. When he wailed in the early morning hours, we turned the house upside down to find missing pacifiers. When we finally got him to calm down in his crib after a long day, we crawled out of his room on our stomachs to avoid being seen. When he was being weaned, we drove for miles in the car to make him drowsy enough to fall asleep without a bottle.

The lack of sleep was only part of the challenge, and gradually every hour of the day became affected in some way. As with all new mothers and fathers, we discovered once you start having kids, there's no going back to your old way of life; like it or not, you're changed forever. By the time we moved again, the permanency of the situation had started to sink in. We had no choice but to keep persevering, however, and one slow step at a time we started to get the hang of being parents.

As we settled in at Fort Lewis in Washington State for our last assignment, we sensed we had come full circle. Several years before we had left home and family, feeling young and inexperienced; as we returned to our starting place in the Northwest, we had not only grown up, but also brought back a child of our own.

After Fort Lewis and nearly five years in the Army, we moved on to the civilian world. The transition was difficult, but we made it through and things once again settled into a routine. We began to get a few full nights of sleep and felt increasing confidence in our ability to raise a child. As the memories of the infant years began to fade, we entered a very risky period in the life of a couple: the time when young parents begin to forget how hard the first baby had been. Robby needed a playmate, we reasoned. Besides, hadn't we heard two were hardly more work than one?

We had plenty of time to laugh about that statement as we once again stumbled around a darkened house with little Eric. Our only consolation came from already having a full list of techniques to lull him to sleep.

Balancing kids, money, and a new job stretched us very thin over the next few years, yet we made it. The raising of children almost completely filled our time and drained our energy, but as before, we relied on each other and pushed ahead day by day. Months and years began to pick up speed, and before we knew it, the oldest was in first grade and the youngest in pre-school. Our babies, it seemed, had grown up before our very eyes.

It occurred to me one day that Betsy and I were turning a corner of sorts. *Who are we now?* I wondered. I hadn't had much time to think about that particular question since Robby was born. We were definitely not the same two people as when we started. We had set out on our grand adventure ten years before with nothing but hope and love and each other. With the passage of time we had grown up a lot, and changed.

When a couple first starts out, sometimes it seems as if the world determines the course of their journey; they step out in a certain direction, then momentum takes over. Without giving it much thought, they end up doing the same things everyone else is doing: finding a job, having kids, doing their best to get ahead. A lot of couples work their way through the early years of their relationship on automatic pilot since every day is a matter of survival.

But when the kids start heading off to school, a husband and wife suddenly realize they have time to think again. They have a few choices and can set their own goals.

We've come a long way together, I thought, *and we have so much of our lives ahead of us. Now that we can choose, what's our direction going to be?*

"LOOK, HERE'S ONE that's missing a claw! It looks like he's growing it back, though." Robby was fascinated by the red-orange crayfish clinging to a rock on the bottom of the river, holding fast against the swift current.

We had driven our truck a few minutes away from a favorite camping spot in northern Idaho and put our inflatable raft in at a stretch of deep water on a small river. After floating downstream a ways, we had beached the raft to wade in the tumbling current as it picked up speed along a stretch of sandy riverbank. We had already found several other crayfish, along with frogs, water beetles, and large schools of tiny minnows.

"Grab it," I said to Robby. "That's the biggest one so far."

"No way! It'll pinch me!" He poked the crayfish with a stick and it scooted away, propelled backward in spurts by the rapid curling of its tail. Eric was busy collecting smooth rocks on the bank, arranging them into tidy piles sorted by color. *This is great*, I thought. *What more could you ask for on a camping trip? A lazy afternoon on a river, bright sunshine, and the amusement provided by Mother Nature.*

Both Betsy and I had grown up camping, yet we had never appreciated how much work it must have been for our parents until we hauled our two young boys off to the woods for the first time. In spite of several mishaps on our first few trips, we had kept at it, gradually accumulating the right equipment and rediscovering how to build fires and set up tents. The kids loved camping, as we had when we were young, and it was often all we could afford for a family vacation. With our youngest having turned four in the spring, our trips were getting to be more relaxing and a lot less work.

What could possibly spoil this ideal scene?

"Wow. Those clouds are moving in fast." Betsy pointed behind us and I turned to look. Dark, low clouds were enveloping the nearby peaks, cloaking them with promises of rain. The weather forecaster had said mountain thunder showers in the afternoon, and here they came. The wind suddenly picked up speed as the edge of the front reached us, and the sky darkened overhead.

"Pack it up!" I shouted. "We're going to get it!" Robby splashed to shore and flopped into the beached raft as Eric scrambled to shove as many rocks as he could into the pockets of his shorts. "Come on! There are rocks back at camp!"

Betsy collected the bow line and started to push the boat off the sandbar into the current. We had floated quite a distance and there were several minutes of paddling between us and the safety of the truck.

Eric climbed into his place by Robby as the wind began to give way to the first drops of rain. Betsy was already in her spot at the front, pulling with her paddle, as I gave the raft a final shove into the water and jumped into the back. The boys were silent as we made steady progress through the increasing rain, watching the small splashes rippling across the surface of the river. High rock walls topped by fir and cedar slid by on either side.

The same raft, I thought. *The same raft as ten years ago. A small yellow boat with no built-in sense of direction, and now it is heading upstream, against the current, with no arguments.* Our combined paddling was smooth, natural, and coordinated. And there were two kids sitting between us, being ushered to safety by a couple of adults who had grown slowly but surely into their role as parents. A decade had passed so quickly, yet we had already collected what seemed like a lifetime of experiences.

Uncharted territory. We had been through a lot, and more stretched ahead. But I knew we would make it, because without realizing it at the time, we had discovered the secret to a successful marriage right from the start: we had done everything together. We had made our decisions together, developed our interests together, and learned to enjoy being with each other all the time. It didn't matter what direction we chose in the future, because the same commitment would pull us through.

The last of the wind passed by as the main body of the rain clouds rolled directly overhead. There was a moment of stillness, then the rain pelted us with driving intensity. We continued stroking steadily, Betsy pulling on the left ahead of me, while I used my paddle on the right, or occasionally as a rudder, to keep the back end straight. The truck came into sight around a bend in the river.

The children didn't complain about the soaking, mesmerized by the whitewater dance of raindrops on the river. If you stared long enough, it looked like the thousands of tiny splashes were being driven up from below, as if the water was bristling by itself into a fast, rolling boil. One more short stretch, and we could land the raft on a small beach and scramble up to the waiting dryness of our small pickup.

We've come so far with each other. The adventure is only just beginning, and we can choose to go anywhere we want in the future. I brought the raft's back end around a little to align myself with my wife's course toward the shore. I wondered how it could be that we were paddling the raft with no problems at all, then thought: *Maybe it's because we are so used to working with one another that we can tackle anything with perfect, unconscious coordination.*

Three more strokes to the beach. *Or maybe . . .* the cold rain soaked through to my skin as my mind considered another possible angle. *Just maybe, my wife knew where we were headed from the start.* Betsy looked over her shoulder at me and smiled as we grounded.

And as long we're together, I thought with a grin as I stepped into the shallow water, *that's a lead I can follow any day.*

❖   ❖   ❖

RIDING LESSON:

If a husband and wife turn toward each other first,
it doesn't matter what direction they go after that
because they'll always be together.

THREE DAYS ON THE TRAIL

"ALL RIGHT, BOYS, dump 'em out!"

Our Scoutmaster waited for us to empty our backpacks onto the floor before starting his customary pre-hike inspection. "We've got a long trip ahead of us this weekend, and your pack is going to be the only thing that keeps you alive." Mr. Weldon pulled out his list of essential items and unfolded it. "Or kills you, depending on how much extra junk you decide to bring." We arranged our gear in front of our nylon backpacks and waited for him to start down the row.

"Now listen up. I'll inspect you one at a time by calling out each thing you're supposed to take. You hold the item up, then put it back in your pack. Anything left on the floor when I'm done isn't essential equipment, and you don't need it." Mr. Weldon sounded a bit weary, as if he feared what he would discover in the jumble of camping and hiking gear dumped on the ground. He had been through this many times during his years of Scouting, and knew young boys had a habit of strapping all kinds of strange and unnecessary things onto their backs before hitting the trail.

His concern over the loads we would be carrying was justified in this case, because the trail happened to be a long one. Our hike would carry us through the rugged terrain of central Idaho, following a path that climbed over several mountain ridges in a three-day loop. Any unnecessary weight eliminated now would make the trip a lot less strenuous, especially for the younger scouts.

Mr. Weldon stepped up to the first boy in line and shook his head over the pile of clothing and equipment on the floor. Packing for a long hike is a study in maximum survival on minimum supplies, and it takes experience to master the process. That experience can be gained in only one way — by carrying too much weight over too long a distance. The first young boy was so new to the troop he had only achieved the lowly rank of Tenderfoot Scout, and the pile of supplies lying in front of him made it obvious he had never been on a long hike before.

"Who helped you with your backpack?" asked the Scoutmaster.

The Tenderfoot had a suspicion he'd brought too much gear since his pile appeared bigger than the rest. He looked around at the other scouts, hesitant to admit who had given him advice on packing. After a long pause, he finally said in a quiet voice, "My mom helped me." Mr. Weldon pursed his lips and nodded silently. He'd seen the situation many times.

If a mother supervised the packing process, the result could be dramatic overloading. It came down to maternal instincts — moms just seem to have trouble restraining their natural protective urges when it comes to sending their children out into the wilderness. To Mom, security equals quantity, and every possible hardship must be planned for. The first maternal instinct is to provide plenty of warmth against the chill of the mountain air, and layering is her solution. In a very methodical manner she starts with the skin and works out.

First comes underwear, and the boy is provided for particularly well in this area. He is cautioned to change them daily for proper hygiene, and extra pairs are packed in case he feels the need to freshen up more often. T-shirts, socks, multiple pants, jackets, gloves, and a stocking cap follow. By the time she is done with the bedroom phase of packing, the boy has more layering than an onion. If he actually wore everything his mom packed, he would be able to lose twenty-five hands of strip poker and still be decent.

Yet it doesn't stop with the bedroom. By the time the last zipper has been zipped, the last bulging pocket snapped, and the last extra blanket tied on top, the boy is equipped for an assault on Everest rather than a three-day hike. In reality, he would probably have greater success climbing the world's tallest mountain because he would have the help of several porters to carry his massive pack.

No doubt the Tenderfoot's mother had the best of intentions, but he had so much camping gear it had taken two people to carry his backpack in from the parking lot before the meeting. Mr. Weldon patiently went down his list of essentials with the Tenderfoot, calling off each item as the young boy put it back into his pack. When they were done, enough extra stuff remained on the floor to hold a yard sale.

"All right," said the Scoutmaster, "time for some tough choices. Do you really think you're going to need four rolls of toilet paper?"

"Looks like he's planning to be *wiped out* on the hike!" The words came from Jake, a boy farther down the line. Jake was thirteen, with a couple of years of scouting under his belt. He had mastered the art of packing and could have been a voice of experience for the troop, but he preferred to use his sharp tongue for sarcastic comments. His remarks were often amusing, yet rarely helpful in any situation. "He's got so much toilet paper he could wrap up in it for a sleeping bag," Jake continued. "Sort of like a Boy Scout cocoon." Giggles could be heard from the rest of the troop.

"I'll give him a hand," said a voice that rose above the laughter. The helpful words came from Hank, another thirteen-year-old with a wit to match Jake's but tempered by a quiet, soft-spoken manner. Hank was all heart, and he won people over by his attitude rather than his appearance. He had freckled cheeks, brown eyes, a butch haircut, and ears that stood out from his head like small saucers on either side of a dinner plate. Hank had been the target of Jake's barbed tongue since he'd joined Boy Scouts, and he knew the damage it could cause.

"Oh, great! Hanky-panky is going to give the new kid a lesson on how to use toilet paper!" Jake smirked. He loved to make fun of Hank's name, and he felt pleased with the reaction he was getting from the rest of the boys. "He probably knows what he's talking about—he's full of it anyway!"

"Pipe down, Jake!" ordered Mr. Weldon. "I've got enough to worry about without your nonsense." He addressed the whole troop. "You boys have got to work together on this hike, and those kind of comments don't help anyone." He moved to the next scout in line and started over at the top of his list while Hank quietly began helping the young Tenderfoot sort out his equipment.

By the end of the inspection, the essential gear was repacked and ready for the trip. Mr. Weldon nodded his approval. "Let's wrap up the meeting, boys," he stated as he strapped the troop's first aid kit onto his own load. "Time to go home for your last few nights of clean sheets and home-cooked food."

Success in hiking, like success in life, is often determined by two things: the load we carry and the people we travel with. In my experience, those two factors are closely re-lated — the right people can make our loads considerably easier to bear, while the wrong ones do nothing but increase our burdens. Since this was the Tenderfoot's first outing with the troop, his backpack was going to be hard for him to handle no matter what it weighed. Considering the challenges facing him, the attitude of his hiking partners could easily mean the difference between his success or failure on the long and difficult trail.

The next weekend found our troop in a convoy of station wagons and pickups, heading for the drop-off point at the beginning of the hike. As we drove north, the farmland surrounding our home town gradually gave way to sagebrush, then aspen, and finally pine trees, which thickened from small groups to unbroken stands of timber that covered the rolling foothills. After a few hours, our destination began to rise up from the horizon: the Sawtooth Mountains. The snow-capped peaks were ringed with clouds that shone brightly against a blue expanse of sky. A gentle breeze, carrying the scent of the forest, washed over us as we unloaded our gear.

"It's a fine day for hiking!" beamed Mr. Weldon as he worked his arms through his pack straps. "Get 'em on, boys! We've got several miles to cover before sundown today." Something about the beginning of a hike always brought out a certain exuberance in our leader. It could have been the impending thrill of adventure, but more likely it was the spectacle of young boys struggling to stand erect under heavy loads.

He turned and looked at the Tenderfoot. "How's your friend treating you?"

The Tenderfoot, having inserted his arms into the straps of his pack while seated, was attempting to stand without success. "What friend, sir?" the young scout managed to grunt as he rolled over to his hands and knees.

"Why, your best friend this weekend — your backpack!" the Scoutmaster grinned broadly, giving the young boy a hand up.

"I think his 'friend' is a little too much to handle," laughed Jake as the Tenderfoot staggered over to lean against the support of a tree. "Looks like his mom packed it with extra stuff again after the inspection. In fact, it's so big his mom could be hiding in there right now!" The assembled troop laughed as the object of Jake's attention turned red. Quietly, Hank, helpful as always, stepped forward and tightened up the young boy's shoulder straps and fastened his hip belt.

"Better?" asked Hank. "I'll help you out until you get used to it." He took the Tenderfoot's sleeping bag and strapped it to his own pack before swinging it up onto his shoulders. Slowly the line of boys filed out of the gravel parking lot into the forest. A few of the parents sounded their horns as they pulled their cars onto the road and turned toward home. We'd see them again at the end of the hike.

By the time the sunset filled the western sky, we had traveled several miles to the first overnight stop. Aside from a few blisters, everyone had done well — everyone, that is, except the Tenderfoot. He had struggled from the start with the weight of his pack and the steepness of the trail, his body growing more tired with each step. The only thing that had kept him going was constant encouragement from Hank.

Hank had a very deliberate approach to hiking — and to life, for that matter. He carried his load without complaining while he kept an eye out for other scouts who might need a helping hand. On this trip he had taken a special interest in the young Tenderfoot. Hank's friendly grin and large, sunburned ears were the first thing the overloaded boy had seen at every rest stop.

Jake, on the other hand, had been more interested in getting a quick laugh. He'd noticed the friendship between Hank and the Tenderfoot and concentrated his efforts on both of them. He usually started with Hank, whose quiet nature kept him from talking back.

"Hey, Hank!" Jake had called out as soon as the packs dropped at one rest stop and the boys removed their hats to cool their heads. "Your butch haircut looks better when you're sweating, kind of like someone just watered the lawn!" Hank had ignored the insult. "Can't talk, huh? Probably takes all of your energy to hold those ears up." Jake could be ruthless at times, and after he warmed up on Hank he would start in on the Tenderfoot. In spite of several warnings from the Scoutmaster, the sarcastic remarks had continued for the entire day.

As usual, Hank had kept his silence as long as the unkind words were directed at him, but he always found his voice when the attack was against the younger boy. By evening, the troop made camp on the shore of a small lake. All were tired as they rolled out their sleeping bags, yet the harassment didn't end; as the Tenderfoot unloaded his pack, Jake wandered over.

"What's in there, kid?" He kicked a large plastic bag with his toe.

"Oh, not much," said the Tenderfoot, unaware he was walking into a trap as he emptied the bag onto the ground. "Some stuff my mom packed for taking baths."

Jake smiled. "Oh, really? Taking baths?"

"Yeah. See, she put my shampoo in a little bottle, and here's my washcloths and hand soap. And this here is lotion." The young boy squeezed some into his hand. "I have dry skin."

"I see," Jake nodded, his smile turning into a smirk. "And what's that?"

The Tenderfoot picked up the can Jake was pointing at. "This is powder."

Jake pounced. "Baby powder? Your mom sent along baby powder? Is the Scoutmaster supposed to change your diaper every night or something?"

"Hey, Jake, cool it." Hank walked over as the Tenderfoot started turning red in the face. He took the can and held it up. "It's talcum powder, not baby powder."

"You call it whatever you want," Jake shrugged. "But I say that if a baby is using it, then it's baby powder."

"Why are you making such a big deal out of it?" asked Hank. "It's just part of his bath stuff."

"Well, his bath stuff is as stupid as he is. Who takes a bath on a three-day hike? Real scouts don't even change their clothes until they've been out for at least ten days." Jake smirked again. "Unless their mommy makes them."

Hank began helping the Tenderfoot put the soap and washcloths back in the bag. "Why don't you lay off? He can bring bath stuff if he wants to, and you shouldn't make fun of him." Hank straightened up and looked Jake directly in the eye. "And you shouldn't make fun of what his mother packed for him, either."

"The only reason you're saying that is because you're acting like the kid's mother right now!" Jake laughed. "I say anyone who takes a bath out here is just plain stupid." He turned and walked away.

The Tenderfoot sighed. "I guess it was dumb to bring all this bath stuff, but I didn't know any better."

Hank slapped the him on the back. "Your mom was just looking out for you. Don't worry about it." He walked back to his own pack and stood silently for a few minutes, deep in thought as he looked out over the calm water of the lake. The wheels were turning in his mind.

The next evening, the scouts made camp in a high mountain valley that had been dug by a glacier in the last ice age. The bottom of the valley held several small pools, fed continuously by water melting from the snow on the surrounding mountains. The calm pools looked inviting, and after dinner several of the boys wandered over to assess the possibility of swimming.

One by one, they tested the water with a finger. Liquid ice.

As they turned to leave, Hank strolled up carrying a plastic bag and a towel. "What's up, guys?" he asked cheerfully. All eyes turned to his ever-present grin.

"You're not swimming, are you?" said the last scout to check the temperature. "This water would make your goose bumps get goose bumps."

"Naw," said Hank. "I'm not swimming. I'm going to wash up. This looks like a perfect tub to me." He looked at the Tenderfoot. "Hope you don't mind if I borrowed your bath stuff."

The young boy shook his head. "No problem."

Hank began to strip off his shirt. "Anyone going to join me?"

"You're crazy!" said several of the boys who had tested the water. Hank ignored them as he continued his preparations.

"What's going on?" It was Jake, walking up with the rest of the troop.

"Hank is going to take a bath in this ice pit!"

Jake launched into a fit of laughter. "You're an idiot, Handkerchief! Only a fool would get in there, especially to take a bath. You're as stupid as I said last night!"

"I don't think he's stupid," said the Tenderfoot in a small voice. "I think he's tough."

"He's tougher than me," agreed another boy.

"Me, too," chorused several others.

"He's not tough." Jake's voice was getting louder. "He's the stupidest person I've ever seen!"

Hank grinned broadly and winked at the Tenderfoot as he sat on a clump of grass to pull off his boots. "I can't believe I'm the only one taking advantage of this natural bathtub." He stood up and pulled off his pants. Grabbing his soap, he walked purposefully to the edge of the pool. The scouts watched expectantly as Hank dipped a toe into the water.

"Is it cold, Hank?" someone asked.

"Maybe a bit here on the edge," Hank said calmly and stepped in without hesitation. His grin grew into a big smile. "Ahhhhh . . . feels good."

"Go, Hank, go!" Someone yelled. "What a tough guy."

This was too much for Jake. "I'm telling you guys, he's not so tough. Look, the water's not really that cold, is it Hank?"

Hank was up to his knees. "Not at all, Jake. Feels great." He scooped up some water in his hand and splashed it on his chest. A rash of goose bumps instantly appeared, but Jake wasn't observant enough to notice them.

"See?" said Jake. "I could get in there too, if I wanted."

"Then get in," came a deep voice from the back of the crowd. Heads turned to see the Scoutmaster speaking. Mr. Weldon crossed his arms, and everyone turned back expectantly to Jake.

"I will!" said Jake. He began to strip his clothes off. "Hey, Hank—how is it now?"

Hank was up to his thighs, strolling calmly into the pond as if it were a steaming hot tub. "Still feels great!"

Jake pulled off the last of his clothes and paused. Everyone watched Hank intently, knowing he had reached the true test of water temperature. Toes, knees, and thighs were one thing, but crossing the threshold to the belly was the real measure of a man. Hank gritted his teeth behind clenched lips and took a big step forward. The water lapped up over his navel. It was hard to tell if he was shivering below the rippling water, but there was no sign of a flinch from the waist up.

"Must be a hot spring down here in the bottom," said Hank. "It's getting warmer!"

The ball was in Jake's court. He looked at the calm pool, edged by grass and moss and disturbed only by Hank's progress. Hank was now up to his chest. "Come on, Jake. I'll make room for you."

Jake dipped his big toe in. "Yow!" He yelped and jumped back as the shock of the frigid water traveled up his foot. He quickly looked around. All eyes were on him. "Hey, Hank. It's, uh . . . a little chilly here by the bank. You say it's better out there?"

Hank was lathering up his soap. "Oh, yeah. It's really warm here in the middle."

Jake had talked himself into the difficult position of getting in the pool or losing face in front of the whole troop. Since the toe test confirmed the water by the bank was icy, his only hope was that the pool really was warmer in the middle. And for that he had to rely on Hank's word. Try as he might, he could think of no way out.

Jake decided to take a leap of faith. Literally.

He backed up ten feet from the edge and crouched into a sprinter's start. Taking a deep breath, he charged at the pool and jumped as high as he could, his body looking as white as a plucked turkey as he cut a long arc through the air. Jake had good form until half-way through his flight, when he suddenly lost his nerve. In a flurry of kicking legs and pumping arms he attempted to reverse course in mid-air, but his struggles were useless, serving only to twist his body backside down before he hit the icy water. He disappeared beneath a huge splash.

A split second later he shot straight from the bottom into the cool evening air as if he were a submarine-launched missile. Gasping frantically, he dog-paddled through the icy pool toward the bank, then scrambled out and lay huddled in a shivering ball on the wet grass. Laughter echoed from the assembled group as Hank waded calmly out. His legs were a lovely shade of blue, but his disposition was as warm as ever.

With a smile that spread from ear to ear, Hank looked down at his tormentor and chuckled. "Gosh, Jake — you just needed to give yourself time to get used to it!" Calmly, he wrapped a towel around his waist and picked up the bag of bath items. He started to walk away, then turned back and dug something out of the bag. "Hey, Jake," he said, dropping a can next to the shaking boy. "If you don't want to take a bath, maybe you can just freshen up with a little baby powder."

Hank gathered his clothes and strolled back to camp, followed by the beaming Tenderfoot and the laughter of the rest of the troop.

In the morning there was less talk than usual as the scouts walked the last few miles of the trail. It would take more than one cold bath to change Jake's personality, but for once he kept his thoughts to himself. For the first time, however, the Tenderfoot was all smiles. His load seemed lighter, and there was a bounce in his step. Bringing up the rear, walking along at his usual steady pace, Hank was also smiling as he strolled through the bright rays of a mountain sunrise. As the troop walked out of the forest a couple of hours before noon, the station wagons and pickups were lined up in the parking lot and the Tenderfoot's mom was waiting expectantly with the rest of the parents.

We're all on this long journey through life together, and hiking partners make all the difference. Depending on who we're walking with, the trip can be a lot of fun or it can be miserable. Look around to see who might need some assistance, and remember a kind word and a helping hand are always appreciated. As far as packing goes, try to travel light without overlooking the essentials. And if there's any doubt about taking the bath stuff, ask yourself this question: what would your mother want you to do?

❖   ❖   ❖

RIDING LESSON:

Nothing we do to help someone else is insignificant. Every act of kindness, no matter how small, will affect the course of a person's life in some way.

A Star is Born

"FIFTH AND SIXTH GRADE boys' chorus tryouts on Tuesday," the sign by the office announced.

I read the words again, an idea beginning to form. *This could be it,* I thought. I had just started the first week of my fifth-grade school year, and I was looking for a way to make myself known. An image of me standing in a spotlight on stage began to take shape in my mind. *This could be my ticket to popularity.*

By that time in my school career, I was already getting the inkling I would never achieve fame through my accomplishments in sports. The situation was not completely hopeless, but my coordination skills did not seem to be developing at the same pace as my peers'. To put it another way, I wasn't *always* chosen last when teams were being selected, just often enough to send a clear message about my classmates' assessment of my athletic ability. But chorus . . . there was something I might have a chance at—an activity requiring no coordination at all.

Why I entertained the notion that performing on stage would be my ticket to celebrity status I'll never know, yet it is possible my name had something to do with it. My last name, Weigle, always set me apart from the crowd. Aside from making me last in every alphabetical line that didn't include a Zimmerman, the spelling invited all kinds of fun pronunciations: "Wiggle," "Wyglie," "Weeglie," "Wijjle," and a dozen other imaginative articulations. I learned to answer to anything starting with a "W."

I discovered early on the pointlessness of trying to reason with my childhood peers, though I tried to explain in the simplest terms I could. "*Why-gull.* It's pronounced Why-gull," I would patiently begin. "You see, it's German . . . ." It took me a few years, but I finally realized the same thing everyone with a unique name eventually figures out: other kids don't have the slightest interest in pronouncing it correctly. What fun would that be?

No matter how it was pronounced, my name made me stand out. Maybe the knowledge I already had a noticeable last name led me to think I could capitalize on it and achieve real fame—sort of an Engelbert Humperdinck approach. I just needed to find an activity that could really benefit from such a distinction, and the boys' chorus seemed to be the perfect opportunity.

There was only one small problem: I couldn't sing. There wasn't much musical ability handed down in my family to begin with, and my sister, Anne, hogged up almost all of it. She could sing like the proverbial canary, but all she left for me was scraps. Even today, when the congregation in my church stands to sing, my wife has trouble getting any words out because she is biting her cheek to keep from laughing. For some reason, she finds my manner of singing humorous. I have explained to her that changing key with each new line of a song only means I have a flexible voice, but she doesn't buy my story. She has diagnosed me with an unstable sense of pitch and a complete lack of rhythm.

"I used to sing in the Army every day when we were running," I have reminded her. "And my soldiers told me I sounded great."

"Your soldiers were just kissing up. And that wasn't singing, that was yelling." Always the realist, my wife, yet I must admit that when it comes to singing, I couldn't carry a tune if it came with contoured hand grips.

So you can imagine my surprise and great joy when I was selected to be in the fifth and sixth grade boys' chorus after only a brief tryout. *I'm a baritone!* I discovered, feeling proud as I stood on the stage for our first practice, missing the fact that everyone else who had tried out was also selected.

That's the way it is when we're chasing a dream — we get so wrapped up in the possibility of success our minds ignore inconvenient details. On the one hand, that's a good thing because it keeps us going, and as long as we keep going we'll eventually achieve one of those crazy dreams. On the other hand, inconvenient details are sometimes warning signals that we're about to do something foolish, and ignoring them can result in significant embarrassment. But at my first practice, I was oblivious to the possibility I might not be as good as I imagined. I concentrated instead on my desire to become a famous vocalist.

Our teacher was an idealistic young man who must have gotten lost in Idaho on his way back from Woodstock. That's not easy to do, and probably indicated he was in the midst of a really bad trip. Needless to say, he appeared a bit out of place in our small town. In addition to misguided faith in our ability, he had three distinguishing characteristics: a pony tail, granny glasses, and a passion for late 60s and early 70s music. One of the boys referred to him as "Mr. Hip" when he turned his back, and the nickname stuck — at least when he wasn't in the room.

We were a rough-sounding bunch, although we did have volume going for us. We made hamburger out of every song we sank our teeth into, but boy, could we belt them out.

The goal of our twice-weekly practices was to prepare for the big fall concert, our first exposure to the unsuspecting public. Our repertoire was made up of contemporary songs, including hits such as "The 59th Street Bridge Song" (more commonly known as "Feelin' Groovy") by Simon and Garfunkel, and "California Dreamin'" by the Mamas and the Papas. I started to believe we were pretty hot, at least in practice, and I began to dream of the glory that would be mine when our show opened.

During the fall of that year I spent a lot of time on the tractor after school, using it to rake hay and do other work in the fields. I sensed the importance of rehearsing — probably because Mr. Hip started stressing it the first time he heard us sing — and the tractor happened to be a perfect place to practice. It was a small, green John Deere with no cab and a very loud two-cylinder engine; I could sing at the top of my voice without anyone hearing me over its constant popping. People driving by probably wondered why the idiot in coveralls and boots was hopping around on the tractor, but in my mind I was a star. Nothing could keep me from chasing my dream of fame in the spotlight, and with my brain fogged up by tractor exhaust, I sang my heart out to an audience of corn, field mice, and the occasional sheep.

I don't remember all of the words to the songs, yet I do recall standing up with the wind in my hair and dust in my teeth to belt out the choruses. *You know,* my addled brain thought after a few weeks of sucking down gasoline fumes, *I am feelin' pretty groovy! This concert could be my big chance. The only thing I have to do to stand out from the other guys is sing a bit louder and throw in a few cool moves. I'll be the star!*

I was in luck, because "California Dreamin'" was perfect for descriptive arm movements. I developed a whole routine involving everything from subtle nods to waving my arms in the air over my head. Before long, I developed the delusion I could even dance a little. *Heck,* I thought, smiling to myself as I practiced a hip gyration, *if I don't watch out, they may ask me to do a solo next time!*

The night of the big concert finally arrived. Peeking through the curtain behind the stage, I could see Mom and Dad finding their seats. The school gymnasium, which doubled as the cafeteria when the basketball hoops were cranked up out of the way, was filled with dozens of brown folding chairs, all facing the end with the short three-step stage. Off to one side sat old Mrs. McDaniels, ready and waiting at the keys of the upright piano. *Oh my gosh! There's a lot of people out there!* My heart started to pound in my chest.

"My stomach hurts. I think I'm going to be sick." I looked around to see the source of the voice. *Oh, great.* It was the kid who stood right behind me on stage. Fear was beginning to spread like a disease through the entire group.

"I'll sing louder if you want to just keep your mouth closed," I offered helpfully. He gave me a stricken look and wandered away to sit on the wrestling mats rolled up along the back wall.

"Okay, boys! Let's do our warm ups," shouted Mr. Hip, clapping his hands to gain our attention. "Sing with me: may, me, my, mo, moo. And louder: may, me, my, mo, moo." He continued through our regular warm-up routine while the audience filled the gym, scraping chairs on the other side of the thick curtain.

173

The time had arrived. Silently we filed onto the stage, taking our assigned places. From my spot in the second row, I could see Mom and Dad sitting in the middle of the crowd. *Can they see me?* I wondered. I would have been hard to miss, because that night I was the epitome of a 1975 fashion plate from head to toe: blue suede hush puppies, purple-hued polyester shirt with psychedelic patterns, clip-on tie, brown corduroy flare-leg pants, and a thick leather belt with a big wooden buckle that my aunt had bought for me in Mexico. I had done my best to dress like a star, and I felt quite proud of my snazzy appearance. Looking at myself in the mirror before leaving home, I imagined that girls would be swooning at the very sight of me.

Mr. Hip walked out last and stood in front of the crowd, hands clasped behind his back. As he went through his brief introduction, I took a few deep breaths and gave myself a pep talk. *Okay, Scott, this is it. You've got the clothes, you've got the moves, now you have to do your stuff. Just like on the tractor. It doesn't take much to stand out from the crowd; these people will be eating from your hand.* I looked across the sea of faces. *But, boy, there sure are a lot of them, aren't there?* My heart started thumping in my chest again.

Mrs. McDaniels smiled at us from underneath her poofy wig and began pounding out the first song. Something was wrong; my body would not respond to my brain. No matter how hard I tried to force it to do a little shuffle, a hand wave, or even a nod, it refused to cooperate. Unconsciously, I fell into the same movement all the other boys were doing: a side-to-side swaying motion with arms locked down to their sides. *What's wrong with me?!* I thought. *I'm blowing my chance!*

The first song ended, then the second and third with barely a quiver from my fear-stricken body. In fact, the only gestures from anyone in the group were coming from Mr. Hip, who was lifting his hands repeatedly, palms up, as he hissed "Louder!" over and over again. After so much exuberant singing in practice, he was becoming exasperated with our performance, since he seemed to be conducting a chorus of swaying mimes.

Finally, we came to the last song, good old "California Dreamin'," and my last chance at a dramatic start to my singing career. I felt loosened up by that time and figured I could manage some physical movement. Since nothing below my chin was responding, I decided to concentrate on winking. *I'll let my eyes do the talking,* I thought, alternating from left to right. *I'd better exaggerate them so they are visible all the way to the back.*

Half-way through the song, I noticed Mom and Dad were staring at me and whispering. *I'm beginning to have an impact!* I thought, gaining courage. *I'll try nodding my head.* I forced my chin to perform one barely perceptible nod, when suddenly a commotion broke out further down the line in the front row.

In spite of repeated warnings from Mr. Hip, Dusty Morgan had violated the first rule of boys' chorus: he had locked his knees. As a result, he was bent over at the waist, staggering around like a drunken rhino and threatening the first row of the audience. It could have been comical, yet the danger to the spectators was very real; Dusty happened to be a big kid, the tallest one in class, and the first faint shadow of a beard was already showing on his cheeks. While it would cause only a minor bit of excitement if he nose-dived into the lap of an adult, the younger brothers and sisters in attendance wouldn't survive the encounter. Parents scrambled to shield their children from harm as Mrs. McDaniels, oblivious to anything but her piano playing, continued to bang out musical accompaniment to Dusty's headlong charges.

Just in time to avoid serious injuries, Mr. Hip sprang into action. He must have had practice reviving staggering people at Woodstock, because he knew exactly what to do; hooking a shoulder under Dusty's chest, he forced him into an upright position. The lumbering giant of a boy instinctively sucked in a breath of air and opened his eyes. Guided by Mr. Hip, he shuffled back to his place in time for the last chorus of the song.

The concert was over. As we walked off the stage, I realized I had blown my first shot at a singing career. How could I compete with Dusty's dramatic performance if I couldn't even move my body? Behind the curtain once again, I listened to the girls' chorus harmonizing through their routine. Compared to us, they sounded like a choir of angels. *Oh well,* I thought, *at least no one threw up on me.*

"What was wrong with your face during the last song?" Dad asked in the car. "It looked like you were in pain."

In pain? I tried to explain. "I was, uh, winking . . . you know, in time with the music."

"Well, you looked like you had a twitch," said Mom. "Don't do that again, okay? It worries us."

Fall had given way to winter, and it was too cold for tractor work. That removed my opportunity for rehearsal, yet it didn't matter since practicing hadn't actually improved my performance. As a group, however, we did improve in at least one respect; inspired by Dusty's unfortunate example, at the spring concert we all made sure we flexed our knees throughout the entire show. Instead of swaying mimes, we looked like swaying, bowlegged mimes, but at least no one passed out.

Dreams. Dreams of greatness, of success, of fortune and fame: these are the dreams that fill the heads of young people—and every adult I know of. Unfortunately, as we age our dreams often die a slow death from lack of exercise. If you find that's been happening to you, it's time to recall a few of the crazy pursuits of your youth and remember what motivated you to stick your neck out. That same attitude may be enough to get you moving once again down the path toward your goals.

My crazy dream, the delusion I could sing, stayed with me until high school, where they had real tryouts for chorus and I couldn't even make the first cut. Yet a seed had been planted, and perhaps that brief time on the stage kept alive my desire to keep chasing my goals as I grew up, no matter how wild they might be. I moved on to other pursuits as I got older, looking foolish doing all sorts of things until I found something I was good at.

It took a lot of failed attempts, but I learned that when it comes to dream chasing, we're never finished until we quit, and looking stupid never killed anyone. *Being* stupid can be fatal, but simply looking stupid only makes you *wish* you were dead. Take it from someone who has performed on stage in a purple polyester shirt and a clip-on tie — you can survive any embarrassment.

Aside from instilling a desire to keep chasing the spotlight, my chorus experience taught me another important lesson: don't lock your knees. You may have to perform for a long time before you get your big break, and you'll never go the distance if you don't relax and breathe. If you have trouble loosening up, try throwing in a few dance moves — they may not make you famous, but at least they'll keep the blood flowing to your head.

❖　　❖　　❖

RIDING LESSON:

Chasing dreams and looking foolish are often as inseparable as smoke and fire. If your actions aren't as publicly visible as a column of smoke on the horizon, then your fire has probably gone out.

AN ANGEL
I COULD BELIEVE IN

"YOU ARE NOW entering Ranger country."

I stared through the window of the taxi at the words painted in gold on black rocks by the side of the road. The statement should have been followed by the words: "And you will never be the same again."

I felt completely alone, in spite of other soldiers in the cab. *What am I doing here?* I wondered. I had been able to put my fears aside during the long airplane flight from Idaho to Georgia, but they pushed to the front of my mind as we passed more of the black rocks. *I hope I'm good enough to make it.* I shook my head as we pulled into the Ranger compound. *Why did I want this training so badly?*

Every year, about sixty ROTC cadets from colleges across the nation were given the opportunity to attend the Army's elite leadership course at Ranger School instead of the usual summer camp. For me, earning the black and gold crescent of a Ranger tab was the fulfillment of a dream I'd had since starting officer training my freshman year. Being able to sew a Ranger tab on my Army uniform would mean I had passed a test that most people would hesitate to take. I began the application process for the school in the spring of my junior year, and the day I received my acceptance letter was one of the most exciting of my life.

I had no idea what I was getting myself into.

When college ended for the year I had a few weeks at home to gather the items on the packing list and work on my physical endurance. Ranger headquarters was located in the heat of the Deep South, so I ran during the full sun of midday to prepare myself as well as I could. The time passed quickly, and before I felt ready I was dragging my duffel bags through the small airport in Columbus, Georgia. Within minutes, sweat beaded on my forehead from the oppressive humidity.

"Where you goin', sir?" It was the same question the cabby had drawled to thousands of soldiers as they stepped off the plane on their way to the "Home of the Infantry" at Fort Benning.

"I'm going to Ranger School," I replied, still not believing I had arrived after so many years of thinking about it.

"Got a whole cab full." He pointed to a yellow station wagon filled with duffel bags and shaved heads. "You can split the ride to Harmony Church."

I didn't know if the Harmony Church area of Fort Benning was named after an actual church, but I did know it was the location of Ranger School headquarters. The cabby threw my bags in with the rest and I joined the quiet crowd in the taxi. We took a back way that wound through the thick pine forests of the training base, and soon the black and gold rocks began to appear at the side of the road, warning signs that we were entering the stronghold of a proud military tradition. No one spoke as we pulled up to the headquarters building.

Nine weeks, I thought as I shouldered my duffel bags. *I can do anything for nine weeks. Can't I?*

The first week was for cadets only. We lacked the experience of the regular Army soldiers, so the extra training was designed to teach us a few basics and toughen us up. The fun started immediately—we were awakened by exploding artillery simulators tossed under our barracks at three o'clock the first morning. Ranger instructors in black T-shirts screamed at us to jump out of bed, and we ran to get in formation in the gravel parking lot with no time to dress. As my dog tags bounced against my chest, I looked around and realized I was the only one not wearing Army-issue brown boxer shorts; instead, I had gone to bed wearing baggy red civilian shorts.

Striving to stand out in a crowd may be a good plan in some circumstances, but not there. A sergeant yelled at me to elevate my feet on the side of the barracks to perform the first of hundreds of pushups I would do throughout the course. *If cadet week is this bad,* I wondered as I ground my palms into the gravel, *how much worse can the real Ranger School be?* The answer, I would soon discover, was "a lot."

Cadet week represented my first exposure to the method used by Ranger School to teach leadership under stress. It was explained to us that the Army could not simulate the fear of death in combat by shooting at us—the instructors said this as if it disappointed them—so they had to exaggerate other stresses to make up for it. This was accomplished by allowing only a few hours of sleep a night and reducing our food ration to about one and a half meals a day.

The sleep and food intake were carefully calculated to be just short of what was needed to sustain us through constant marching with hundred-pound loads on our backs. The extra measure of endurance, they said, would have to come from our mental desire to persevere. Meanwhile, students would be rotated through leadership positions and graded on their ability to execute a variety of missions.

The concept seemed good on the surface, but after experiencing it, most of us agreed we would have preferred being shot at.

As cadet week drew to a close, I had the sinking realization I wasn't ready. The real course, which lasted fifty-eight days, hadn't started yet, and I could already tell it would be more than I had prepared for. My body was having trouble adapting to the rigorous demands being placed on it, and I lacked understanding of many military procedures. I was there, however, and could do nothing but make the best of it.

At the first formation of the actual school, the cadets were mixed with regular Army soldiers. Standing at attention while names were called to form squads, I saw an earlier Ranger class marching by on the way to graduation. They had made it through the course, which should have given me hope, but two things bothered me. First, the group appeared to be only half as big as ours. Their failure rate, I'd heard, was typical. Second, they were thin—really thin—and looked exhausted.

Fifty-eight days, I thought. *An eternity. And this is day one.*

My squad of ten marched to the barracks to set up the gear we had been issued. The squad was composed of every rank from private to captain, but I couldn't tell who was who. Nobody wore rank in Ranger school, and all uniforms were stripped clean of everything except a name tag and a "US Army" patch. Leadership in this course was expected to come from strength of character and not from the privilege of rank.

I struggled to put together my rucksack—the Army's name for a backpack—according to the packing list. The tangle of straps and buckles attached to my frame looked nothing like the example the instructors had shown us.

"Here, look at mine. Just roll up the straps and put a thin strip of tape around them."

I looked up at the soft-spoken voice. It came from a young man, about five-foot-nine like me, but thinner than my medium build, with fine features and blond hair. His name tag said "Elder," and his rucksack looked perfect. "I'll help you get it right." He squatted next to me and held out a roll of green duct tape. "My name is Frank."

Frank Elder was a private from the elite First Ranger Battalion, stationed at Hunter Army Airfield near Savannah. He didn't fit the image I had always assigned to a member of a Ranger battalion, but I knew the soldiers in those units were the best of the best; only a few years had passed since they had made a parachute jump in combat to spearhead the invasion of Grenada. The three Ranger battalions practiced tough Infantry skills on a daily basis, yet every member still had to go through Ranger School and earn his shoulder tab. Their lowest private knew more than any cadet ever could, and I was grateful for Frank's help.

"Thanks. Thanks a lot," I mumbled. I couldn't do anything for him in return, but his assistance was given willingly and patiently, without a trace of pride.

We finished my rucksack in time for another formation; "city week," was about to begin. The first seven days of instruction, based at the Harmony Church headquarters, were designed to prepare us for the skills we would have to demonstrate throughout the course. The long days started with a six- or seven-mile run before dawn, then continued with a full training schedule: hand-to-hand combat, bayonet fighting, map and compass navigation, obstacle courses, survival swimming, classroom instruction, and more.

By the end of city week we had already lost several dozen men from our class, victims of the constant physical and academic testing. Frank and I were still hanging on, and our squad was drawing closer together under the pressure. On the seventh day, we marched out to Camp Darby, a remote training site in the pine forests on the edge of the base. There, the leadership training would begin with evaluations of our ability to conduct patrols.

In theory, patrols comprised an effective way for a military unit to accomplish a variety of missions. Conducted at night, patrols were always supposed to be a stealthy, camouflaged advance into enemy territory. That was the theory. The Ranger School reality was an overloaded, staggering stumble of exhausted and hungry students, trying without success to stay awake while the rest of the world slept. Over and over, we practiced three types of patrols against the enemy unit opposing us: reconnaissance, ambush, and raid. Every student would be called upon to be leaders in graded positions during each phase of the course, and we all had to pass our quota of patrols to earn our Ranger tabs.

We were pushed hard at Camp Darby. The missions, some starting with parachute jumps from helicopters, became more and more complex. Everyone was assigned to a "Ranger buddy," and the two men were supposed to look out for each other day and night. A few pairs made it all the way through the school together, but my partners kept failing one test or another and flunking out. Never my official Ranger buddy, Frank was always there to lend a hand to anyone who needed it, and I needed it a lot.

Next, we traveled to Camp Merrill, near Dahlonega in northern Georgia, for the Mountain Phase. We were entering the long middle stretch of the course, and although it seemed as if we had been in training forever, the end was still more than five weeks away. Before we began patrolling the high ridges of the Chattahoochee National Forest, we received mountaineering instruction. Each student had to pass a knot test and successfully complete several rappels down a sixty-foot cliff. We lost a few more soldiers to injuries as they attempted to slide down the face of the slippery cliff while carrying stretchers, packs, or other students.

We were also beginning to lose men from the results of prolonged exhaustion and insufficient rations. Our immune systems were weakened, and any infection could progress rapidly into a serious condition. Tiny, burrowing insects called chiggers infested the pine needles on the forest floor and could chew a path for infection directly into our skin; we were issued small bottles of iodine and cautioned to treat bites immediately.

Our thoughts turned constantly to fantasies about food. I began a list of favorite dishes in my pocket notebook and planned to ask Mom to fix every one of them the day I returned home. The other great fantasy was sleep, an often-forbidden pleasure we pursued like addicts. In the early hours of the morning, it was an easy bet the only ones awake were the students who were being graded. Everyone else slept in any position, and it was not uncommon to see a man suddenly fall flat on his back, pulled over by the weight of his rucksack as he dozed on his feet.

Sleep deprivation also brought on hallucinations, and accountability became a nightmare. No flashlights were ever allowed and movement had to be accomplished in strict silence. On moonless nights, it was nearly impossible to see the soldier ahead of you in the darkness, and we struggled to stay in touching distance during the long marches. The job of keeping track of the men in the patrol fell to the student assigned as platoon sergeant. All night long, this unfortunate soul could be seen counting up and down the line of men, checking to be sure no one had gotten lost. A break in the line could often be traced back to a student standing behind a tree or bush, imagining it was a soldier while the rest of the unit patiently waited, or slept, behind him.

No one was immune from the effects of hunger and exhaustion, no matter what kind of experience they brought to the course. Like me, Frank had lost about fifteen pounds and had to struggle to do his part on every mission. By the time we walked out of the rain-soaked mountain forests for the last time, the constant patrolling had taken its toll. Each morning, I felt pretty certain I could make it to sunset, but there were no guarantees after that. Next stop: Desert Phase.

The long flight in the Air Force C-141 Starlifters from Georgia to Fort Bliss was spent, predictably, in sleep. The stomach-lurching roller coaster of low-level flight awakened us an hour away from the drop zone on the Texas-New Mexico border; the pilots were practicing hugging the mountainous terrain to avoid enemy radar. In the back, airsick students began to regret eating the greasy, fried chicken in the box lunches we had been issued before take-off.

Straining to stand erect in the lurching plane, we struggled into our parachutes and strapped on our rucksacks and weapons. Desert Phase, a week-long patrol with no classroom instruction, was to begin with a parachute assault onto a dry lake bed. Airsickness spread quickly through the plane; as soon as one soldier lost it, everyone began to retch. Anything would be better than the heat and foul air of the cargo jet, and we tumbled thankfully into the bright desert sun soon after the doors were opened.

I landed on Desperation Drop Zone in a cloud of dust. *Hot*, I thought as I rolled up my parachute, *but at least it's not humid.* Buses took us to our staging area in a parking lot on the edge of the scrub-covered desert, and we began planning for our first patrol. Looking out at the distant horizon, I realized the dry bushes of the White Sands area of New Mexico reminded me of the endless clumps of sagebrush in Southern Idaho, and I began to feel homesick.

How am I going to do this? I thought despondently. After the desert, we still had the Jungle Phase in Florida to complete. Students had to pass at least half of their patrols to graduate, and I was at fifty percent. I had failed one at Camp Darby because of poor performance and passed one in the mountains only by sheer luck, I felt. The missions were getting harder, and my thoughts must have showed on my face.

"What's wrong?" Frank asked quietly. We were sitting together under a poncho shelter, rigged to provide some protection from the blazing sun.

"I wasn't ready for this, and I feel like I'm in way over my head," I confided. "How do you keep going? This Ranger stuff is so hard, and you do it all the time."

He laughed. "Well, for starters, they feed us a lot more!" He smiled briefly at the thought of food and I studied his thinning face. Frank had gone into the Ranger Battalion right out of high school and was younger than my twenty-one years. But experience counts for a lot, and I had looked up to him for guidance nearly every day. In contrast to my agonized expression, his looked peaceful.

He must be so confident, I thought. *He's done all of this before.*

"You know, I'm afraid, too. Every day, I don't know if I'll be able to make it." Frank was looking straight ahead, at the horizon.

"You?" His statement surprised me. Frank had a slight build and narrow shoulders, yet he could carry any load you put on him.

"Yeah. I don't worry so much, though. I know I'll be strong when I need to be." He took a drink from his canteen, then offered it to me.

"No thanks. How do you know you'll be strong?"

Frank turned to look at me. "Because I believe in Jesus."

"Oh." I hadn't expected that. "That makes you strong?"

"All the strength I need. All I have to do is ask."

In his soft voice, Frank told me of his conversion to Christianity. His story had begun a couple of years before, when his girlfriend had left him soon after he joined the Ranger battalion. That may not sound like a terribly tragic event, yet to a young man away from home for the first time it had been a shock. He felt depressed and absolutely alone as he walked through the dark streets of Savannah one night, wondering how he would find the strength to keep going.

As my inner thoughts showed on my face as we sat in the desert, Frank's desperation must have been evident to anyone who had seen him. A car had pulled up to the curb next to him, a door opened, and a group of young men invited him to church. Without knowing why, he jumped in, and found the strength he had been searching for. With the strength came faith—faith that God would give him whatever he needed to handle any challenge, including the rigors of Ranger School.

As he spoke these words, Frank's features glowed with an expression I had not seen on a young face before. I listened to his story in silence, yet I wasn't convinced; my thoughts were too full of the agonizing details of my immediate problems for me to think of a larger perspective. *If anything is going to get me through this mess,* I thought, *it will be my own effort. That's the only strength I've ever relied on.* But his words lingered in my mind as we heaved our rucksacks onto our backs and filed out of the parking lot toward the brilliance of a desert sunset.

Finding our way became particularly difficult in the flat desert. Because there were no mountains or valleys to show up as landmarks on the map, we had to navigate strictly by compass and an accurate pace count of the distance we had traveled. It was a challenge to keep on the straight line of a compass bearing while weaving around the large clumps of brush, and we ended up hundreds of meters off track on nearly every mission.

One of those missions was mine to lead, and, as I had feared, mine to fail. I was down by one patrol, and I had to pass one in the next part of the course, Jungle Phase, or flunk out of Ranger School. My sense of hopelessness grew with each passing day, even through the excitement of the desert live-fire exercise. As machine guns rattled and 60 millimeter mortar shells exploded on the distant target, A-7 Corsairs roared overhead as our air support. It was the first time I had experienced the full power of military weapons, yet I could think only of surviving the last few weeks and going home.

We walked back from the desert after seven days of patrolling and slept on the concrete floor of an aircraft hangar. Army regulations stated soldiers had to have eight hours of sleep before a parachute jump, but they didn't say anything about a bed. A few hours later we were pitching and rolling once again as our jet transports hugged the low terrain on the approach to the next drop zone. I could tell I had arrived back in the South as soon as my parachute opened; the heat and humidity of Eglin Air Force Base surrounded me like a wet blanket as I dangled over the training area in the Florida panhandle.

Two more weeks to go.

We received a few days of instruction in a variety of jungle operations, including snake identification, traveling by raft, rappelling from helicopters, and river crossing. Then we went back into the bush for our final graded patrols. Some of the students who had been thin to begin with looked almost like skeletons. Conversations about food were constant, and I can remember one soldier captivating an audience for fifteen minutes as he lovingly described, in detail, the breakfasts his mother made.

"And I'm going to ask her for French toast the first morning I'm home," he declared in a businesslike tone as he perched on a stump.

"Does she serve it with butter and powdered sugar?" I asked, remembering my own mother's breakfast table.

He looked directly at me without blinking and said in a deadly serious voice, "She makes it any way I want it." We all nodded our heads solemnly as if he had stated one of the fundamentals of life. Food was our biggest obsession, and we could talk about it for hours at a stretch.

Jungle Phase brought the most complex operations yet. Heavily armed Specter aircraft, parachutes, helicopters, rafts, and Navy landing craft off the Gulf Coast were part of our planning for patrols. Coordinating the details of transportation proved difficult, but the real challenge came when we hit the ground and walked off into the bush, straining under the weight of rucksacks loaded with blank ammunition. Nearly every mission involved a traverse of a wide stretch of swampland and a dangerous river crossing in pitch-black darkness.

By the fifth day in the jungle, I had been pushed to the limit of my endurance and I felt doubtful I could handle even one more challenge. That night, our mission took me over the edge. The hours from sunset to sunrise have lived in my memory for over a decade, coming back time and again with memories of what happened . . . and with memories of the strength of Frank Elder.

We hooked up our rappelling ropes as soon as we boarded the four UH-1 "Huey" helicopters. My rope lay coiled in a burlap sandbag on my lap as we lifted off the asphalt landing strip and flew into the darkening sky. The formation of aircraft surged over the treetops, washing the leaves in the downdraft from the rotors. *Just like in a movie,* I thought, watching from the open door.

I could see three helicopters flying nearby in the glow of the sunset. They seemed motionless in relation to me, yet the ground below was speeding by in a blur. Whenever the formation of aircraft banked into a turn toward my side, I could look down across a hundred feet of space and see other Ranger students sitting in open doors under whirling rotors. The bright ribbon of a river passed under us like a shining highway.

We slowed to a hover. A sergeant slapped the back of my helmet and shouted a command. I threw my sandbag hard enough to clear the helicopter skid and watched my rope stream out as it dropped into a small clearing. At the next command, I swung my feet out and balanced backward on the skid under the swirling rotor blades. The sergeant pointed at the student next to me and the helicopter bobbed as he kicked off. A moment later came my turn and I felt the friction of the rope burning through my leather gloves as I tried to slow my rapid fall. I hit the ground hard, landing on my back, then scrambled to the edge of the clearing.

The helicopters thumped into the distance as my squad joined our platoon on the shores of the nearby river. Silently, we loaded into rubber rafts and pushed into the current.

What would my friends think of this? I wondered. The helicopter flights, parachuting, and rafting seemed so glamorous from a distance, but while actually doing them all thoughts were focused on what would happen after the ride ended. One man filled everyone's canteens as we paddled silently along, dropping iodine tablets into each one to purify the murky water.

After about an hour on the river, we bumped into the shore and dismounted. Frank and I laid next to each other on our bellies, pointing our weapons outward to provide security against attack. A few minutes passed and a whisper came down the line. Time to rotate leaders. Frank dragged his rucksack to the location of the Ranger instructor and received his assignment: platoon sergeant.

We already knew where our mission would take us, since we had been briefed before boarding the helicopters. Our route began directly ahead in the swamp a few feet from the river bank. Silently, we staggered to our feet under the weight of our rucksacks and filed into the darkness of the dense vegetation. Frank knelt at the edge of the clearing, touching each man as he walked by, counting us by feel to make sure no one got left behind. Immediately, the water began to rise over the tops of our boots, and the only sound was the plodding squish of our footsteps.

I had not been assigned to a leadership position, so I had nothing to do that night other than survive. However, I felt exhausted, and the effects of the constant patrolling were catching up to me. Right away, I had trouble keeping track of the student ahead of me, in spite of the "cat eyes" sewn on the back of his cap. Every soldier had them: two small rectangles of luminescent tape, charged up in the daylight so they would glow at night. They helped near the beginning of a mission, but slowly faded as the hours of darkness stretched past midnight. I struggled to keep up, reaching constantly to touch the rucksack in front of me to find my bearings as the water began to lap up over my knees.

"Seventeen!" A hoarse whisper came from behind me. Frank, from his position at the end of the line, had initiated a head count. If each man was paying attention, the relay should end at the front in an accurate count of the students in the platoon. The platoon leader at the front would then radio back to Frank that all were accounted for.

"Eighteen!" I whispered hoarsely into the darkness ahead of me. I didn't hear the next number, and whispered again. "Eighteen!"

Suddenly, I realized I had allowed a large break in the line to occur. I ran ahead, tripping over a log and stumbling into waist-deep water. Forcing my way across the pool with no consideration for the person trying to follow me, I scrambled up through the brush on the muddy bank and ran into a rucksack.

"Eighteen!" I whispered again, and this time I heard the next number passed ahead. The line of soldiers continued into the night, and I slid down into another deep pool of murky water. I was climbing over a tangle of slippery logs when I heard a hushed voice behind me again.

"Fifteen!" Something was wrong. Either the head count had ended at the front in the wrong number, or had never made it. For whatever reason, Frank had started another one, and it was already off by the time it reached me. Or, just as likely, the first one had been off.

"Sixteen!" I whispered, and heard the next number whispered ahead of me. I pulled my foot from a tangle of fallen vines and pushed slowly through the water; the muscles in my legs were starting to ache from the effort. I heard a splash behind me, and a firm hand gripped my shoulder.

"Seventeen." It was Frank, counting his way up the line to make sure everyone was present. I could barely move through the slime, yet there he was, carrying the same load as I and staggering ahead twice as fast. He scrambled through hanging branches to the next student, then the next. *Something is making him strong tonight,* I thought, remembering our talk in the desert. *A lot stronger than me.*

An unknown amount of time passed and we made slow but steady progress. I heard counting again, this time from up ahead. It was Frank. Having made his way to the front, he was now double-checking the number by counting us as he returned to the rear. *He's not going to let any of us get lost in this swamp.* The thought of his strength was enough, barely, to keep me moving. I wasn't going to let my friend down, since he was trying so hard for us. *Trying so hard,* I thought, *for me.*

The cycle repeated itself at least two more times that night; the attempted head count passed up from the rear, followed shortly by Frank, scrambling forward almost at a run to confirm it, then doing the same thing in reverse as he went back to his position at the end of the line. I could barely force my way through the quagmire once, but with his back-and-forth running, he accomplished it three times or more. We finally climbed up a sloping bank onto drier land, and there he was again, quietly counting us out of the swamp as we filed past on the way to complete the mission for the night. All present, all accounted for because Frank Elder had faced the same conditions as the rest of us and risen above them to fulfill his duty.

Frank's example of strength in the midst of the swamp is my final, enduring memory of him, for just when I thought I couldn't take any more, my ultimate test began. Already one patrol short of the fifty percent pass requirement when I completed Desert Phase, I never made up the loss. A few nights later I failed a leadership position during another jungle patrol, which meant I had to pass two in a row. I struggled successfully through an ambush as a squad leader, which gave me some hope of graduating. Then came my final chance to achieve the patrol quota as platoon leader on one of the last missions of Ranger School.

And I failed, miserably. In the darkness of a long night, I tried without success to overcome two months of hunger and exhaustion in a mission that remains a blur of confusion and mistakes to this day.

Our failures live in our minds far longer than our triumphs, for some reason, and this one was especially significant. It was the first time in my adult life I had truly been tested in a situation that mattered, and I had come up short. I heard my name called out during the final formation, and I fell out to the rear, forming a line with the others who hadn't made the grade. Two days later, the rest of the class,

Frank included, boarded buses and began the long trip back to Georgia to graduate. A pit formed in my stomach as I watched them go. I felt utterly and completely alone.

I was a "recycle." I had gone through the worst physical experience of my life in the swamps of Florida, yet I had to do it again if I wanted to graduate. Starting over with the record I had coming out of the desert, I had to pass only one patrol to achieve fifty per cent—but I had to go through Jungle Phase all over again to do it. Nothing in my life had prepared me for facing up to such a large failure due to my own inadequate actions. I was paying the price for not being good enough, and I replayed my final, failed mission in my mind over and over again, mentally punishing myself for not performing correctly under pressure.

Do I keep going or quit? A few recycles made the decision to drop out. But the embarrassment of going home without a Ranger tab made me stay.

I was assigned to a squad in the next class that came through. Within a few days, I faced another river crossing, another night in the darkness of the swamp, another test. And the first thoughts of Frank came back to me. When I thought I couldn't take another step through the mud, I suddenly felt his presence, his example, in my mind. I desperately needed strength to keep going, to keep moving ahead, yet I didn't know how to ask for it. I thought of Frank, and the image of a man who had the strength of his faith was enough to pull me through. Somehow, one grueling step at a time, I made it, passing my final patrol. I felt exhausted, physically, mentally, and emotionally.

Back at Harmony Church, I shook my head at the formations of new students we marched past on our way to graduation. Three long months had passed since I had been one of the newcomers. As my father pinned the black and gold Ranger tab on my left shoulder, I thought of Frank Elder once again. I didn't know it at the time, but a pattern had been established. Although Frank had been unaware of anything beyond simply doing his job, his actions in the swamp became an image that was never far from my thoughts whenever I faced a difficult challenge.

I returned to my senior year in college, hoping I would meet him again, somewhere, some day.

LATER THAT SCHOOL year I was home on a break from my final classes before graduation. My older brother was on leave from his new position in the Army, an assignment at Hunter Army Airfield, Georgia. Knowing his unit supported the First Ranger Battalion, I told the story of Frank Elder and the example he had set for me in the swamp, hoping Brett might know the friend I had made the previous summer.

Brett listened silently, a strange look on his face. When I finished, he hesitated before speaking.

"I don't know how to tell you this, Scott, but . . . ." his voice trailed off for a moment before continuing. "Private Elder is dead."

"Dead?"

"Yes. I went to his memorial service. I'm sorry."

It was my first experience with the hard reality of a military career. The Army, and all the services, practice a dangerous game: the preparation for war. In the pursuit of realistic training, sometimes people died. But Frank?

"How?" I whispered, disbelieving.

"On a river crossing, at night. He slipped away from the guide rope in the darkness and drowned."

When Brett got home, he sent me a copy of the program from the memorial service. There it was in black and white: my friend from Ranger School, my example of strength, my inspiration in times of hardship—gone. He had perished in a situation hauntingly similar to the long night in the swamp in Florida. Reading the program, I realized he had literally died trying.

And now, I thought, *I'll never see him again.*

Or would I?

RANGER SCHOOL HAD been hard, yet at least it had a definite ending. Soon after college, I found myself permanently enrolled in the school of life, with continuous testing but no graduation in sight. Family life mixed with Army life, and financial challenges mixed with time commitments. The real test is always the mental one; at some point as we struggle forward, carrying ever-heavier responsibilities, we realize we're in for the long haul, and we don't know when the journey might end. Like the swamp, the water gets deep sometimes, and the footing gets slippery. As I moved forward in my life, the events of Ranger School wouldn't leave my mind.

Having succeeded in earning my Ranger tab should have been enough to make me forget my mistakes, but it wasn't. I simply couldn't rid myself of the taste of failure. In every difficult situation in the years that followed, the hollow pit in my stomach returned, and I relived the dark night of defeat in the swamp and the judgment of my own conscience telling me I wasn't good enough.

Time passed, and life got harder for me after I left the Army and started over again at the bottom of a new career. Financial pressures mounted as first one child, then another needed clothes to wear and food to eat. My hours were stretched thin to cover more and more commitments, and the hardest part came from having dreams of my own I wanted to achieve but seemingly no time to pursue them. The trail to the success I envisioned was hard to see, harder to follow, and stretched ever-longer away from me.

Yet at the lowest moments, when I felt I couldn't take another step, I thought of Frank Elder and lifted my head. In my memory he was tireless when I felt tired, and concerned for my welfare when I felt too sorry for myself to care. Where was he leading? I didn't know, but it was somewhere up ahead, and the thought of him gave me enough strength to take one more step.

I began to search for a deeper answer, somewhere outside myself and my own efforts, because I was growing more and more weary of trying. One day, unable to continue any further on my own, I raised my eyes and said, "Please, God, don't leave me alone."

And the answer came, unspoken yet clear in my mind: *My son, I never did. I touched you when you were tired, guided you when you were lost, and counted you as one of my own. I led you, one step at a time, out of the darkness and into the light. From the moment you first needed help, and before you knew how to ask, I was there. My son, I have never left you alone.*

And then I understood: God had been with me the entire time. Even when I didn't want Him, He had found a way to guide me, slowly but surely, through the most difficult times of my life and into His light. Frank Elder had entered my life and lived in my mind because God, in His wisdom, had given me an angel that an unbeliever could believe in.

Life is still hard, but my load is lighter since I am no longer burdened with the failures of my past, and the strength I have been given is enough to share with others. When I could finally lift my head and look beyond my own needs, I noticed there were so many people struggling as they tried to walk forward by themselves, staggering under a heavy load as I had once done. I began to reach out to family, friends, and others. I shared a smile, an encouraging word, a helping hand, and I received in return the reward of watching another person take one more step or make it through one more day, maybe when they thought they couldn't.

You can rest now, Frank, because I have made it through the swamp and nothing is too hard any more. It is my turn to be accountable, to lead others by example through the darkness of their trials. To touch them and count them in the night, whoever they may be, and urge them forward one more step until they, too, can find the light.

It is my turn to be an angel.

❖　　　❖　　　❖

RIDING LESSON:

We're never alone unless we choose to be.

THE HORSE
KNOWS THE WAY

AS A YOUNG GIRL, my mother used to watch out the window each evening, waiting for her father to return from a day of work in the fields. As the sun dropped toward the horizon and shadows lengthened across their land, she would see him in the distance, driving his team of horses before him along the path to the barn. My mother's father— whom I called Grampie—owned two huge Percheron draft horses that pulled plows and wagons across his southern Idaho farm. They were his steady and reliable companions, and many of his days were spent listening to the slow plodding of their huge hooves from sunrise to sunset.

Mom would run to meet him down at the bottom of the pasture, where Grampie would lift her high up onto the shoulders of one of the large horses. She would grab the harness collar tightly and pretend she was driving as the team walked the last few steps to the farmyard. Even though her small hands could never hope to control those giant animals, there was never any danger of her being carried astray — the horses knew the way and she always ended up right where she belonged, riding gently along the path to the safety of her home.

When I first realized that life is like being on a horse, I noticed a lot of people were experiencing a faster ride than I was. They seemed to be more successful, racing toward their goals with a swiftness I couldn't achieve. I didn't want to be left behind, yet I couldn't go any faster — the mount I was on simply wasn't made for speed. That was when I started to look at my past and realized my mother's story might be showing me a better way to live.

You see, my farming ancestors weren't expert riders, yet they did have plenty of experience with horses. Not the racing breeds, but the workers — draft animals that had the power to pull heavy equipment while still being gentle enough to carry the smallest of children on their backs. If life was like riding a horse, then I knew this was the type of mount that could take me to my dreams: a workhorse, not a thoroughbred.

Thoughts of my mother's evening rides came to me frequently as I examined the stories from my past. I could see her clearly in my mind's eye, a little girl in a white dress, smiling as she perched on the back of a plodding giant. Thinking of her, I began to understand that my own ride through life might not be as fast as some people experience, but as long as I stayed in the saddle and kept pushing ahead, my progress would be steady. As I got to know my own "horse," my attitude slowly changed and I stopped wishing for a faster one. Instead of racing against other people I started down a personal trail where speed didn't matter, setting off to define my own goals and pursue my own dreams.

When we aren't so concerned about other riders we find we have a lot more time—time to notice the scenery along the trail, time to enjoy our families, and time to think about the best way to achieve our goals. I've learned a lot about what it will take to ride to my own dreams, as well as how to make the most of the trip. I'm sharing many of these fundamentals in this book, yet if I had to name my three most important riding lessons, they would have to be these:

First, there's work. Nothing worth having is gained without it, plain and simple. It doesn't matter if we're talking about home improvement, raising kids, or building a better life—we have to be willing to put in a lot of time and effort if we want to accomplish anything at all. It's not always easy and it's not always fun, but I wouldn't trade the lessons I've learned from work for anything in the world.

Next, there's love. Not just a warm feeling for the world in general, but the real thing: love for the people we meet every day in life. Our families and friends need us, and whether we admit it or not, we need them, too. I'll be the first to confess that some people aren't easy to love, but the challenge is good exercise for our hearts.

Finally, the most important thing of all: we've got to have faith. We're going to find some stretches of our trail passing through difficult terrain, and to make it over the rough spots we need faith in ourselves, faith in the future, and faith to carry us through when the whole world seems to be against us. I tried to rely on my own strength for many years, but it was never enough. Ultimately, I found the only thing that works for me is faith in God. It has only been His presence in my life that has given me enough strength to keep riding day after day toward my goals. If ever we find ourselves growing weary from the difficult stretches of the trail, there's help available—all we have to do is ask.

Work, love, and faith: three keys to a successful life. I'm not completely sure where my dreams will ultimately take me, yet I do know I'm enjoying the trip a lot more than I used to. Sometimes the pace is faster, sometimes slower, but it's all part of learning to ride.

So how does a person decide what his or her goals are? Not surprisingly, that question can be answered only by each rider. However, if you don't know exactly where you're headed, let me share one more important discovery: *your horse knows the way.* That's right—your life has a mind of its own, a spirit that drives it, and a certain place it wants to go. It might take a while to figure out where that is, so it's best to get started right away. The sooner you begin to examine the lessons of your past, the sooner you can stop racing against other people and ride off toward your real destination, the place you are meant to be.

The world is filled with constant change and we can never truly get off the horse—but we *can* learn to ride through our lives better than we ever imagined. Instead of wishing for a different mount, let's turn the ones we have into the steady and reliable companions that will take us to our dreams. Then sit back and enjoy the trip. There's no danger of being carried astray, because just as surely as that strong and gentle giant carried my mother to her home so many years ago, the horse will find the way.

God bless you.

My Story

I STRONGLY BELIEVE that everyone's life is a story — a story as exciting, sad, joyous, and hopeful as anything we can see at the movies. I hope this book has caused you to see the interesting plot twists of your own life, and perhaps inspired you to share some of them with another person. Now that you've finished the last chapter and are about to go on with your own adventure, I'll leave you with a few notes on *my* story, just to set the record straight.

There are many characters from my life who have been presented with their real names, because I thought it was important. Frank Elder is one of these, God bless him, and of course my family. Others are actual people, but I have called them by different names, leaving to them the option of coming forward to claim their well-deserved fame or good-natured embarrassment, such as the case may be. If you recognized yourself in these pages, allow me to thank you now for your excellent sense of humor.

Other characters in this book represent more than one person—sort of like a whole scout troop being rolled into a few mischievous boys. There have been so many people who've contributed to my life that there was room for them to speak only if they shared one voice.

Some characters represent something else entirely: the different surroundings within which I have lived my life—the background for my personal story, so to speak. You'll see them if you look closely, and you'll recognize them for what they are: a small-town way of life; the rich heritage of farming; the proud discipline of the Army. These characters and what they represent are as real to me as any people I have ever known.

Like the characters, the scenes all work together to tell my story. Interesting things happen when you bring memories to life, especially when you combine them with the wisdom gained from hindsight. A storyteller lives in his own mind a lot, thinking and re-thinking the meaning of an event, and sometimes it comes out on paper a bit differently than the way it happened in real life. Things have to be communicated in a certain way, so days in reality sometimes compress to minutes on the page, while a momentary flash of insight takes a whole chapter to explain. But that's the way it is in my mind, so that's the way it is in my stories.

Is everything true? Yes . . . in its own way. It's true to the important things I've learned so far in life, true to the people I've met, true to the places I've seen, and true to the organizations I've been a part of. Believe me, it all happened, one way or another.

And that's my story.

Look for this book at your favorite bookstore, or contact the publisher directly to place an order. Letters to the author may also be sent to this address.

Thomas-Kalland Publishers
PO Box 8376 / Spokane, WA 99203-0376
Telephone: 800.788.5476 / Facsimile: 509.455.6858